Dulcie Domum's

BAD HOUSEKEEPING

Dulcie Domum's
BAD HOUSEKEEPING

Sue Limb

Illustrations by Marie-Hélène Jeeves

FOURTH ESTATE · *London*

First published in Great Britain in 1990 by
Fourth Estate Limited
289 Westbourne Grove
London W11 2QA

First published in paperback in 1992

7 9 10 8 6

A catalogue record for this book is available from the British Library

ISBN 1–85702–066–9

Typeset in Bembo by York House Typographic, London
Printed and bound in Great Britain by
Cox & Wyman Ltd, Reading, Berkshire

For Debbie and Ben Johnson,
who committed
matrimony in 1990.

May they never dwindle
into Spouses.

one

Awake in the midst of passionate dream about Roy Hattersley, and wonder why had never noticed before how delicious he was. At length pillow beside me observed to be empty: Spouse evidently already deep in Seventeenth century, downstairs. Cannot blame him.

Throw back duvet (must change covers this month) and gaze remorsefully at what used to be firm young belly. Must get round to post-natal exercises this year. Children burst in demanding crisps for breakfast and realise with sinking feeling that it is still half-term.

Health Visitor calls to make developmental assessment of Harriet, now she is three. Harriet not entirely co-operative. H.V. enquires if she can count to ten and Harriet replies *Not today*. Tempted to boast that she can count to thirty-nine, and sometimes thirty-ten, but heroically refrain. H.V. asks if Harriet can eat with knife and fork. Cannot face revealing that she does not even bother with a spoon, now, and has gone back to fingers even for soup.

Health Visitor produces small box containing tiny car, cow, cup, etc., retires to far end of room, and whispers, 'Harriet, can you pick up the cow? 'Harriet picks up car instead, indicating, in the opinion of the H.V., hearing problems. In my view, method theologically unsound, not allowing for Free Will, the superior attractions of motorised transport, etc. At height of hearing test, hailstorm bursts upon us, and I begin to suspect Health Visitor of speech impediment.

'She may need grommets,' was the verdict.

Harriet, who had slipped away to bottom of garden cries, 'What are grommets? Are they to eat? I want one now.'

Must say, thought grommets were disreputable family in The Archers.

Tea for Health Visitor afterwards. Offer home-made cake. Hope it still counts as home-made if made in another home and bought from W.I. stall. Halfway through tea Henry runs in, stark naked, turns his back to H.V., bends down, pulls both cheeks of his bum apart and presents his anus to her, as meticulously as the lens of a camera. Feel simultaneously horror, and a conviction that I have long wished to do the same myself. For a moment aghast silence prevails. Then Henry remarks,

'I was going to fart, but it seems to have gone back in.'

'Go to Your Room,' I thunder, 'Get Dressed and Wait for Me There.'

'I think I need to drink some more Coke.' Henry concludes, departing.

'He must be a Handful,' observes the H.V. wryly. A handful seems a very meagre quantity to relate to Henry. Were the hand of the Almighty Himself to burst through the clouds, helpfully cupped like an insurance advertisement, I doubt whether it could contain, in the penal sense, my son and heir.

Although *heir* is nowadays purely theoretical. After the H.V.'s departure I brood gloomily on our finances. Spouse's regular forays to the U.S.A. to lecture on Historiography useful, but not conclusive, source of income. (What is Historiography, by the way? After ten years of marriage am too embarrassed to ask.) My own contribution to the Privy Purse extremely fitful. At critical moment, my Publisher rings up and asks whether I would like to write 'a big fat book with a lot of bonking in it.' Odd that he has not noticed my tendency to produce small, thin books with none. Wonder if I can rise, or perhaps sink, to the challenge. What, for example, is bonking? If it is what I suspect, fear that I shall have to dredge the remote recesses of memory to come up with any convincing details.

In midst of crisis of conscience, agent phones to confide enormous (by our standards) advance offered for bonking book. Accept immediately. When Spouse emerges from his lair, inform him we are once again in a position to engage domestic help: news he receives with a shudder. During tea Spouse seems abstracted. Suspect he is still lost in Historiographical conjecture. Wonder if it hurts.

At bedtime reflect that though at lunchtime Roy Hattersley was still trailing clouds of glory, by six he had Gone Ordinary. Does this show the fragility of the erotic in the face of

Coca-Cola

fiscal and domestic convulsion? If so, prospects for Bonking Book bleak. Spouse still downstairs wrestling with the Levellers, so go to sleep hoping for dream about Gorbachev.

two

AWAKE IN MIDDLE of night convinced that Gorbachev has map on his head, and that therein lies Rosicrucian clue to destiny of mankind. Creep downstairs to my study and compare favourite Gorbachev pin-up with world atlas: conclude the famous Mark of Blood is a map of Florida, though not sure whether nuclear installations are represented. Mysterious. Is Florida to be flashpoint of Armageddon? Or retirement home for Gorbachevs, post-Perestroika? *Dunpurgin'*?

Suddenly hear burglarious footsteps in hall: seize *The Rape of the Lock* as most appropriate book to brain burglar with, and tiptoe out to confront Spouse brandishing *Love Sex and Marriage in 17th Century England* with similar intent. Conclude both hungry and quarrel over single remaining banana before hastening back to bed.

Awoken three minutes later (or so it seems) by Henry jumping on my head and roaring, 'How do they make paper do they make a sort of custard out of trees first?'

Harriet constipated. Crouch on bathroom floor for hours whilst she, enthroned, engages in bio-metaphysical speculation. *Is Poo Nice or Nasty? – Discuss.* Rather like papal audience esp. as have faint memory of ancient papal chair constructed rather like a lavatory so misogynistic cardinals could glance up from below and admire the papal credentials. Harriet would make excellent old-style Pope: greedy, tyrannical, sensual. As I am pulling her knickers up she strangles me with expert ease. No doubt Borgias oft did same.

Knock at door heralds Mrs Body for interview as Mother's Help: cheerful, eager and sensationally ugly. Settle her in sitting room and run upstairs in search of Spouse. Joint decision essential to forestall future hostilities. Run him to earth in children's room pretending to mend cot. Urge him to descend and promise him that she resembles Robbie Coltrane in drag, wearing glasses. Then realise with thrill of horror that baby intercom is turned on and Mrs Body downstairs must have heard all. Scream and hide in wardrobe. Spouse shows rare surge of resourcefulness and comments clearly into microphone that he doesn't think *my cousin* looks like Robbie Coltrane, at all.

Still shaking when enter sitting room, but relieved to find that Henry is performing ear-splitting series of B52 bombing raids upon the beaming Mrs Body.

'Stop That At Once!' I cry gratefully, hoping it has gone on for some time.

Mrs Body so cheery that engage her at once, though do wonder if her evident inability to close her mouth may irritate me in the end. We part in rapturous anticipation of Monday, when she starts.

In the afternoon Spouse takes children to park: my chance to start Bonking Book about rich people. Need heroine. Curious inability to remember any girls' names. By half-past-four have written *Charlotte Beaminster was* . . . and am exhausted.

Then remember have never got round to planting bulbs. Seize bulb-planter still in its cellophane – adorned with picture of scantily-clad nymphet planting bulbs with no apparent physical exertion whatever. Encouraged, grab croci and commence. Soon conclude nymphet's soil of talcum-powder softness and abundance, unlike our rock and clay. Vigorous screwing of bulb-planter from side to side necessary. Torture to palms. By time Spouse returns, have developed stigmata and saintly rictus of pain. Spouse unimpressed by stigmata and by *Charlotte Beaminster was* . . . Evidently feels he has wasted afternoon.

Henry asks me if he can make a nuclear submarine out of the marrow imposed on us by Mrs Twill in August and ignored by us ever since. Puzzled by marrow's apparent inability to biodegrade like other helpful vegetables. Instead marrow obstinately persists. Suspect decommissioning may be necessary. Give Henry permission to make two canoes from it, or African masks, or anything non-violent. Henry loses interest.

Make deeply unpopular supper from marrow, and retire, hoping for dream of canoeing through Everglades with Gorbachev. Instead endure nightmare: Pope enthroned: resembles Mrs Body and Robbie Coltrane. Am invited to inspect the Papal credentials and am confronted with monstrous marrow, which explodes, etc etc etc. Reflect Saturdays always difficult.

three

Mrs Body's first week as cleaner, concluded with loss of only three cups, two glasses and transparency of windows. Admit when I discovered soapsuds in Hoover had moment of acute angst in what I think of as Futility Room. Hoover has also lost its ability to whip its lead in like an alarmed snake skittling into a crevice. Lead now lolls slackly on ground. Fight off feeling that Mrs Body has killed my vacuum cleaner, and round her pay up recklessly to compensate for guilt at buried resentment.

At the end of week discover mysterious, but familiar, lack of money in purse. Drive to Cashpoint where receive insulting electronic lie about account and five freshly laundered tenners. Drive home, enter house, and find Harriet and Mrs Body in hall admiring strange dog which has appeared from nowhere and resembles George Eliot.

'Let's keep it!' cries Harriet dangerously, embracing both germ-infested ends of dog at once. Ignore this, pay Mrs Body, and request Spouse to take her home as driving to the Cashpoint was more than enough for my nerves. Convinced that God, if exists, does not mean us to drive at night.

'Can I have the car keys, then?' demands Spouse with impatience. Keys have vanished. Not in usual place on hall bookcase: not in handbag or pocket or car. Get hot. Spouse tight-lipped, fetches spare set, and departs.

Almost supernatural sense of dread rises: is God trying to prevent fatal accident? Would feel irritated if Spouse were to die behind my back with Mrs Body. No grandeur in it. Prefer Spouse to die with Mrs Gorbachev, and rehearse brief funeral in snowstorm with Gorbo offering strong arm to self, pale and dramatic in large black hat. Gorbo and Garbo, in fact.

Hauled back to reality by rogue idea that Mrs Body may be a kleptomaniac. Sit on stairs and feel sick. Wish had asked for references. Harriet seizes opportunity presented by my inertia to disembowel handbag with thoroughness of Drug Squad. Remember mysterious lack of money in purse, and wonder if that also attributable to aforementioned kleptomania. Cannot remember where handbag was during day, but then, cannot remember where I was either.

Renew search, and am prone with arm stuck up behind radiator when Henry arrives home from tea with friend. Harriet finds Tampax in handbag and flourishes it crying 'What is this?' Unaccountably thunderstruck and can offer no explanation whatever. Watch in paralysed horror as Harriet and Henry unwrap it.

'It's a toy mouse,' says Harriet. 'Not a very good one, though.'

'No, silly!' says Henry. 'It's for cleaning guns. I've seen Julian's Dad do it. I didn't know you had a gun, Mum.'

Son and heir regards me with brief moment of respect. Reply that I have many unsuspected attributes, instruct children to see dog off premises, and withdraw to prepare dismal soup of all left-overs in fridge. Realise later including stale slice of apple pie was a mistake.

Whole evening plunged in gloom because of loss of keys and persistent requests from children to keep dog or see my gun. Spouse radiates disapproval about keys and ransacks poor handbag even though it has already suffered six times. By 9 p.m. children safely horizontal and mute, so wander into study and contemplate, with disgust, rudimentary beginnings of Bonking Book about Rich People. Have heroine: Charlotte

Beaminster, but am unable to imagine any details of a life saturated in wealth.

Pick fingers and gaze into night. Suddenly have vision of George Eliot on her hands and knees gazing in out of the dark, imploring me to discard pulp fiction and recover my artistic integrity. Spine actually tingles before I realise it is the dog, returned.

At 11 p.m. Spouse puts head round door and says rather sheepishly, 'Sorry old thing but the keys were in my jacket pocket all the time. You must have given them to me without noticing.'

'Without *either of us* noticing,' I amend sharply, and manage to enjoy a feeling of triumph for two minutes before starting to feel sorry for Spouse in his dejection.

Spouse conciliatory for rest of evening (twenty minutes) but still could not get him to admit that Glasnost is anything more than a cynical publicity stunt.

four

CHILDREN BEING MYSTERIOUSLY self-sufficient in attic: chance for me to penetrate Miltonic chaos of desk. Find old letter from Animal Rights' mob, asking me to write to Gorbachev, to thank him for saving whales stuck in ice. Hesitate. Think of twenty-six reasons why letter not good idea. Remember what, when fourteen, I wrote to Adam Faith, and fear a relapse. Then with reckless sense of plunging into swimming pool full of champagne, sit down and seize pen.

Have just written *196 Cranford Gardens* when phone rings. It is Publisher asking for photograph to put in catalogue. Also enquires about progress of Blockbuster. Or, as Spouse now refers to it, Bonkbuster. Am all too aware that wealthy heroine Charlotte Beaminster has been stuck in her jacuzzi for days because I am unable to imagine what awaits her beyond the bathroom door, but deliver glib communique about progress which Publisher swallows. Phone Valerie to ask her to come and take my photo, and return to letter to Gorbachev, uneasily aware that it is more exciting than all 10,000 words of novel.

Wonder how to address him. Mister? Comrade? President? Darling? Thwarted in my musings by arrival of Mrs Body, accompanied by teenage daughter, Tracey, with Vowel Trouble. She informs me she is studying *Ashtray O'Fart*. Is this a kind of soothsaying, akin to tealeaves and auras, practised in certain down-at-heel Dublin bars? Turns out to be History of Art. Enquire if she likes Bernini: Tracey says she finds it expensive and prefers The Dog and Duck.

Children descend from attic looking important, and leave them watching *Neighbours* whilst Mrs Body has a good go at the bathroom. Hope no enduring psychological damage taking place, to children or bathroom.

Pay brief visit to bedroom mirror and examine face, conscious that ordeal of photography looming. Place both fingers on cheekbones, and pull face back and sideways round behind ears. Vast improvement. Conclude face-lift long overdue and lament that cosmetic surgery against all deeply-held beliefs. Rembrandt's self-portraits, profound sense of individual history, etc. Wonder how much face-lift costs.

Return to letter, and have decided *Comrade* is misleading, *Mr President* too Transatlantic, and *Darling* inadequate, when Valerie arrives to take my photograph. I am placed in basket chair by beech hedge, wrapped in shawls like John Ruskin in old age. Valerie talks about natural light being more flattering. Know what this means, and despair. Adopt what I hope is nonchalant posture secretly intended to pull face sideways round back of ears.

'I don't think I like those hands,' observes Valerie. Feel sorry for hands, and sit on them for rest of session.

Am held hostage by inane grin, fixed but twitching, which always arrives when camera near. As she snaps away, Valerie tells me rather sad story about her neighbours' son who had to lose his big toe, but insisted on burying it in a matchbox, like a much-loved pet frog. Grin will still not go away, but flickers madly like 1950s TV set. Would face-lift feel like that? Perhaps bad idea after all. Want to whistle, if necessary, without danger of ears falling off. By end of photo session, face really tired. Needs hanging in sympathetic dark wardrobe. As, no doubt, will photograph.

Before I can rise from chair, George Eliot appears, wags tail, and lays doleful head on my knee. Children appear, accompanied by Tracey who confesses she is a *raal dag lava.*

'She must be going to be our dog mustn't she, Mummy?' insists Harriet, attempting to mount dog roughly as if it were a kind of furry tricycle.

'She could be really useful too,' adds Henry. 'When you go blind she could be your guide dog.'

Harriet falls off dog into Valerie's camera-case. Murmur excuses and escape to house. Not the first time I have wished the appalling *Neighbours* could have lasted another twenty minutes.

Grab pen, and whisk Charlotte Beaminster from jacuzzi to bathroom window, from which she glimpses new gardener: stocky, balding Slav, with magnetic eyes and masterful manner with turnips. Feel at last Bonkbuster is on the road, and dash off tantalisingly brief note to Gorbachev thanking him for also saving whales, world, etc.

Spouse returns from exhilarating Historiographical Conference in Lucerne, expresses hope that I have got Christmas organised, and remarks that I look tired.

five

SNIFFS OF TV INTEREST in my children's book, *Charley the Chickpea.* Summoned to London for sparkling lunch at which I am to fascinate TV impresario Gerald Thingy and land contract that will make our fortunes. Penelope (agent) insists we must strike while iron hot, despite wretched persistence of school holidays. Mrs Body to hold fort. Tell her that there is a Salmon Mousse in the fridge, at which she looks startled.

Spouse reluctantly condescends to take me to the station, though Levellers have just reached interesting crisis (possibly something to do with gradient.) Harriet produces histrionic scene on doorstep, clinging to my knees and wailing 'Dod't go dod't go Bubby!' NB Wonder if Health Visitor was right about her needing grommets. Yesterday Harriet remarked that *Badeleine's Bubby was baking barbalade* last time she went there to play.

Guiltily conscious of Mrs Body watching scene and forming critical view of my Botherhood. Tear myself away, and recklessly accede to Harriet's demand to bring back 'Sobething bad for by teeth.' Sit in train and fizz inwardly. Cast Clive James as Charley the Chickpea wearing beige boilersuit. London and TV impresario together unbearably dangerous and delicious. Foresee U.S. rights, world rights, second home in Bahamas. Whole experience certainly in the Bad for my Teeth category.

At smart Indian restaurant Penelope introduces Gerald Thingy. Soon notice that Gerald strangely reluctant to discuss *Charley the Chickpea.* Mention Clive James, but Gerald remains inert. Had not realised, in TV world, how swiftly irons can cool. Sombre chill spreads o'er tablecloth. Even Penelope not very lively. Despise Gerald Thingy for choosing vegetarian dish and drinking Perrier, tastes I normally endorse. Part with relief saying how wonderful it has all been.

Find myself afterwards at Oxford Circus, aware that sudden evaporation of TV rights leaves us with a lot less in the kitty. Need for sobriety and good husbandry. Avert gaze from Top Shop and pass by on other side. Pace austerely northwards. Suddenly besieged by ravishing little boutique full of Indian clothes, etc. Dive inside.

Buy breathtaking tropical print dress and four scarves: three fringed, one scintillating pink sequinned silk. Emerge restored. Sod Gerald Thingy. Spineless, chinless and feckless. Despise TV anyway. Idiot's lantern. Instrument of mass anaesthesia. Glad to be in cold winter twilight, strolling alone.

Neck feels cold. Loop dazzling sequinned scarf round neck, hiding most chickenesque areas but not imparting any conspicuous warmth. Never mind. At least neck resembles Goddess's. Knowledge that scarves made in Rajasthan obscurely exhilarating (though later, had qualm about exploitation of Third World labour). Wander through the streets and note the qualities of people. Fairly mediocre, mostly – but forgive them from within my divine neck.

Suddenly realise train leaves Paddington in twenty-five minutes. Plunge into Great Portland Street tube: subterranean hell. Train arrives and doors roll back to reveal human lasagne. Against all instincts insert myself and am carried away. Soon realise am on wrong train. At this very moment train stops in tunnel and switches off engine. Blood rapidly boils. Wish had made will.

Attempt nonchalantly to unwind scarf. Scarf becomes mysteriously tighter. Try again from other end. Asphyxia increases. Am preparing nonchalantly to faint when train jerks back into life. At Baker Street seek Circle train, but There is a Fault. Ten thousand people on platform. Disembowel several in struggle towards exit.

Burst thankfully out into Baker Street and look round for taxi to hail. Taxis with yellow lights seem to have been discontinued. Start to stride to Paddington. Signpost promises three-quarters of a mile. Sure it is lying. Progress impeded by witty little shoes designed to impress Gerald Thingy. Wish had kicked his ass with them.

No buses. No taxis. Sure things would be better in Gorbo's Russia. Moscow Metro carpeted and candelabra'd and no doubt buses every thirty seconds. Convinced will miss train by a whisker. Considering general tendency of BR trains to arrive late, feel that for them to leave on time is hypocritical.

Catch train with ten secs to spare. Travel first sixty miles pinioned between pinstripes, like pound sustained by intense City support. Sure I shall be devalued at Didcot when they all get out.

Remember to remove sequinned scarf just before arrival. Will say it is a Christmas present from Penelope. Harriet hurls herself upon me and I realise I have forgotten the Thing Bad for Her Teeth. Harriet weeps for twenty minutes in car.

At sight of favourite fireside chair, collapse with relief.

Spouse, tight-lipped, hopes I have had a productive day as it has been Hell at Home.

six

IN BED, Spouse reading *Perestroika* which I gave him for Christmas. ('Ah,' quoth he on receiving it, 'an Eastern Fairy Tale.') Eagerly await verdict, but try to concentrate on Conrad. Mind wanders. (Bang goes first New Year's Resolution – sorry, Conrad.) Spouse soon remarks that there are several flaws in Gorbo's historical method. Retort that Gorbo too busy making history to bother with such trivia. Spouse looks hurt. Sink below duvet and bite nails – another Resolution gone. Dream I am Princess of Wales' bosom chum, which affords me great pleasure whilst asleep and intense embarrassment on awakening.

Tracey arrives to take children to town on bus, but confides that her mum has got Sceptic Froat so no chance of any cleaning today. Veil displeasure with sympathy and assure her there's a lot of Scepticism about. Hand over extensive shopping list before withdrawing to study.

Novel still stranded. Charlotte Beaminster's loins have twanged at the sight of sturdy Slav gardener Cherbagov. She is about to wander out to the potager in search of salsify, when I spot a fatal flaw. No husband. Instantly marry her off, to which Charlotte sharply objects. Point out how lucky she is: could be in novel by Hardy and end up blind, drowned or hanged. Husband wrestling with studs in background. Charlotte notices how much more exciting this makes Cherbagov's back, and submits to my creative wisdom. Cannot think of a name for husband, though.

Publisher rings demanding photo requested weeks ago, and threatens if I do not send one to use old one, in which I know I look fat and drunk. Pretend new photos already sent, and curse postal service. Another Resolution disintegrates. Promise to whizz new lot to London instantly. Ring Valerie and timidly enquire about progress of prints. Valerie confides she has Septic Throat, and can still scarcely speak, but will drag herself heroically into the darkroom, etc. Did not think darkroom requires much in the way of vocalisation, but refrain from comment and thank her effusively.

Tracey returns from town with extracts from shopping list, including photos from old film left in camera since August. Perhaps one will do for publisher. Film recalls fête in Dorset village with pretentious old name – something like Peveril St Canonicorum. Fête was at Sheltered Workshop. Shed tear at image of severely handicapped patient, then realise it is badly-timed glimpse of self with sun in eyes and torso mysteriously inflated.

'I can't eat this it looks like sick!' cries Henry of my hastily improvised pasta.

'Tastes like sick too!' laughs Harriet and they launch into endless charade of vomiting which I am too tired to stop. Tell Spouse that holiday necessary to sustain sanity. Spouse replies If you take the children, fine, otherwise Seventeenth Century will go completely off the rails. Must say, thought Seventeenth Century had gone comprehensively off the rails without any help from me. Fear holiday alone with children could be even worse than everyday life. Tracey suggests there are helpful hotels with Clabs and Playgrapes for Kads. Rush out and return with eighteen inches of brochure.

Attracted by Canaries because warm. Spouse frowns and says Madeira would be more the thing. Walks, etc. Dare not tell Spouse that I hope to spend the entire week lying down, and obediently research Walks in Madeira. ' . . . be warned, this path is extremely vertiginous, narrow, wet and prone to landslides.' Go dizzy and fall off sofa. Secretly eat doughnut. Only one Resolution left now.

Sneak back to Canaries ('there has been disseminated even among the barbarians that these are the Elysian Fields.' – Plutarch.) Fear barbarians may have taken over altogether by now but never mind. Warm. Pore over maps – favourite physical activity. Find island called La Palma with capital Santa Cruz, island called Tenerife with capital Santa Cruz, and island Gran Canaria with capital Las Palmas. Lament poverty of Hispanic imagination, and contrast proudly with Leighton Buzzard, Lower Slaughter and Peveril St Canonicorum.

Run to study and christen Charlotte's husband Peveril St Canonicorum de las Palmas de Santa Cruz. Santa for short? No, Peveril. Nice mix of peevish and evil, suitable for obstructive husbands in novels. Roused by his name, Peveril stares out into the garden and snaps, 'I'm going to get rid of that gardener johnnie he looks like a bloody Bolshevik to me.'

Valerie arrives with photos. Try to hide disappointment at evidence that I am no longer twenty-five. Spouse observes that he can see my mother in me. Pre-menstrual tension sets in, two weeks early.

seven

PRE-MENSTRUAL TENSION rapidly spreading over Western Europe. Not looking forward to February either – though have booked week's holiday for self and children on Tenerife at Hotel Dolor de Cabeza in the rapidly developing resort of Forùnculo. We are promised 'British' pub, floodlit crazy golf, bingo, fancy dress nights and personality contests. Can hardly wait, as feel personality has long gone unappreciated. Hotel Dolor de Cabeza also offers magic ingredient: 'supervised children's entertainments.' Intend to lie in shade and let Mrs Gaskell wash over me, whilst children submit to Jesuit discipline elsewhere.

Depressed by begging letter from Newnham explaining that appalling financial burden threatens to reduce them to solitary English teaching post, as opposed to two or three in good old days when there was a choice of shoulders to cry on. Dash off pitifully inadequate cheque and brood blackly on continuing struggle of women's education.

Saskia telephones to wish me a belated Happy New Year. Decide not to tell her I have only one New Year's Resolution left unviolated, nor do I mention Tenerife. She confides that she and Alice are going to Bogota. Make mental note to Bugger Bogota at earliest opportunity, and reflect on the superior opportunities for enjoyment offered by Sapphic lifestyle. Supinely congratulate Saskia thereon, and she rings off in triumph.

Mind slides off sideways in direction of what would be My Sort of Holiday if Sapphic – or even better, Solo. Am wandering in snowy Eastern city – Prague, perhaps. See ghost of Mozart in frosty doorway. Hear bells, see stars. Find cosy little café in which whom do I behold, travelling incognito in dashing fur hat, but . . . Gorbo. He raises his brown eyes, and bang goes my last New Year's Resolution.

Lack of common language no barrier to communion of souls. Within half an hour have convinced him by series of subtle gestures that Decentralisation is the Answer. He nods with that alert and purposeful expression which hath so oft mesmerised me to the marrow, and promises to let Estonia, Latvia, nay, the whole of Eastern Europe, out to play.

Then he seizes my hand and conveys, with a hot stare, that he wishes me to occupy bijou studio flat in one of St Basil's golden domes, as without instant access to my brilliant powers of constitutional analysis his road will be rough indeed. He is just tucking me under a wolfskin on a sleigh bound for a forest retreat when Spouse puts his head round the door and observes that he thought it was my turn to make lunch today.

Run into kitchen and slice onion. Onion has gone dark, and do not blame it. Quotidian existence drab and mankind reeling from succession of disasters. Suddenly convinced that Nostradamus predicted it all. Rush to study and search in vain for Nostradamus, but can only find Nostromo. Spouse puts head round door and asks what the hell I am looking for, not a cookery book he supposes, fat chance of that eh. Cannot tell him it is Nostradamus as he would crow unpleasantly at the very idea so pretend it is Nostromo.

'There it is right under your nose,' he says, 'and now would you mind helping me to feed our children?'

Ashamed, I make Hula Hoop sandwiches for Henry and

Harriet who greet it as Most Brilliant Lunch Ever. Luckily Spouse, immobilised behind *The Independent*, does not notice. Stilton and Bath Olivers disappear round side of paper from time to time, evidence for children of continued survival of their father.

'We want a baby brother,' announces Harriet suddenly in tone of stern industrial negotiations.

'And we want to watch you doing it,' adds Henry. 'You mustn't lock yourselves in the bathroom or whatever you did last time, that's not fair.'

'AND we want to watch the baby coming out,' said Harriet. 'and can I cut the hole in your tummy please, Mummy?' She grabs tin opener and a struggle ensues. Spouse lays down *Independent* and makes a deafening noise which seems to have power to immobilise life. Children hide under table. Wish I could join them. Spouse rises, delivers ultimatum and withdraws to Seventeenth Century. Wonder for a moment if he has a floosie tucked away there – Venetia Stanley, for example. Quite a raver according to Aubrey.

Pick bits of Stilton out of Harriet's hair and wonder if it was a waste of money sending that cheque to Newnham. Do not feel my existence does much to justify women's education. Take children into garden where Henry treads on first snowdrop. Feel it is symbolic somehow, but cannot remember exactly why.

eight

JITTERY ABOUT IMPENDING FLIGHT to Tenerife on Boeing 737. Buy Do-It-Yourself Last Will and Testament at W.H.Smith's. Includes Specimen of How a Will Should be Made: subject Leslie Heath, leaves his Gold Pocket Watch to his son and the rest of his property to his wife. Feel guilty that I do not have a Gold Anything to leave to Henry, but feel sure he would break it within first twenty minutes if I did.

Pack children's clothes. Dear little white shoes of Harriet's with poignant pre-War strap. In flash of precognition see one of them washed up on West African beach. Am afraid that too much sea has to be flown over to get to Tenerife. Should have chosen Istanbul with choice of hundreds of airports en route for emergency landings.

Examine tickets for twenty-fifth time. 'Carrier, Inter European Airways.' Never heard of them. Don't like word 'carrier', either. Reminiscent of bag. Unfortunate memories of what happens when handles give way. Wonder if it is too late to go to Bournemouth instead. Spouse points out Ilminster bypass probably 'even more dangerous than Tenerife airport.'

Suddenly remember worst crash in civil aviation history occurred at Tenerife. Self and children to be in hot, passionate hands of Spanish Air Traffic Controllers. Regret sense of Spanish culture derived entirely from Bunuel films and *Fawlty Towers*. Pray that Air Traffic Controller will not be distracted from his duty by a desire to play cards with priests, perform naked upon the pianoforte, or slice eyeballs. Try not to think of *Fawlty Towers* at all.

Wonder if instead of Spouse as sole heir, should leave whole estate to John Cleese. Cleese certainly contributes more to human happiness on a massive scale. Waste to leave him my pittance though – would probably not even notice it. Feel sorry for Spouse, about to receive devastating blow. What, all his pretty chickens and their Dam. Tell him I intend to insure my life for £300,000, so perhaps that will make him feel more stoically equivocal about our loss.

'Not equivocal at all,' he replies cheerfully. Wonder what he means, and do not like his tone.

Rush to loo and have diarrhoea. Grounds for cancellation? Wonder how much Murdoch would pay for DIARRHOEA THAT SAVED MY BABIES' LIVES with picture of self, enthroned. Emerge pale and shaking and inform Spouse of intestinal malaise.

'Well, you might as well get some practice in,' quoth he. Tone of Spouse's recent utterances lacking in love and sympathy. Resolve to spin revengeful fantasy about Gorbo as soon as I have a spare minute.

Leave study in utter mess, novel stalled at moment when Charlotte's husband announces he will sack sturdy Slav gardener for whom her loins have twanged. Charlotte protests that I cannot leave her in this uncertainty. I shrug sadistically. Serves her right for being so rich.

Feel desperate for reconciliation with Spouse before we part. Must recapture that first fine careless rapture. As soon as children are in bed, carry tray up to his study with cup of Lapsang and small custard tart (his favourite). On seventh stair, trip. Tray performs emergency landing upside down. Arms scalded with Lapsang and nose buried in custard tart. Spouse appears on the landing and asks what the devil I am playing at.

Wipe face in bathroom and conclude perhaps it is better I should die before my resemblance to anxious bulldog is complete.

Lock myself in downstairs loo and consult Tarot about Tenerife. It offers verdict: The Emperor. 'Consolidation of manhood. A man or being of power, honour, worldly knowledge.' Puzzled. Perhaps relaxed by balmy tropical climate, Henry's voice will break suddenly at age of eight. Or have I underestimated moral fibre of Spanish Air Traffic Controllers? Likelihood of meeting own personal Emperor remote: Gorbo too busy in Moscow anticipating urgent date with That Woman. Such a waste the Kremlimousine will whisk him to Downing Street and not 196 Cranford Gardens.

Still, encouraged by outcome of Tarot. Could have been Death or even The Tower Struck by Lightning (Very Fawlty Tower). Intestinal twinges cease, and find I can face Henry's dirty socks, strewn o'er the floor of the Futility Room, with new courage.

nine

SUN SHINES TILL 6.30 P.M. in Tenerife. Bliss. Resort of Forunculo high rise blocks alternating with craters, but agreeable seafront promenade with palms, etc. Hotel Dolor de Cabeza would offend Prince Charles, but room ok apart from small crater under carpet. Henry welcomed into Kiddie's Club – the Dolor-Mites. Harriet rejected though: too young.

'I will kill everybody in this hotel!' quoth she.

Point out, not without secret qualm, the delights of having mummy to herself all week.

Attempt to relax. Sun, etc. But holiday angsts rush to replace workaday ones. Tremble lest Henry and Harriet should get heatstroke, sunburn, Spanish Tummy, be bitten by scorpions, or disgrace me in the hotel dining room (especially that). Harriet obliges on first night by booming above the babble, 'That Fat Lady's eating with her mouth open!'

Fat lady part of large contingent from South Yorkshire W.I. Whole experience like Alan Bennett play with sunshine.

Realise I am only middle-class person in Forunculo. Feel a bit like Perdita, but no sign of even middle-aged Florizel, let alone Emperor as promised by Tarot. Relax and enjoy proletariat as usual. Pleasant not to be urgently questioned about Henry's school, of efficacy of my cleaner. Suspect all other guests here *are* cleaners.

Take Harriet to beach and anoint her liberally with Factor 12 Sunscreen. She immediately rolls in sand and takes on the aspect of a Scotch Egg. Veil myself from Apollo in Tunisian muslin from head to foot. The Turin Shroud relaxes on Tenerife. Rest of Brits on beach are laid out sizzling in rows like sausages under the grill. Entire S. Yorkshire W.I. topless and supine. I don't know what they do to the enemy but by God they terrify me.

After five days of Turin Shroud and Scotch Egg, succumb to hunger for belfries, bookshops, antiquities. Sick of endless bars, cafés, Brits. Baedeker confides details of gracious old inland town, La Rotovata, with carved balconies and Embroidery School. Salivate, and promise Harriet lovely trip in bus and sweeties when we get there.

Long trip in bus driven at speed by someone called Jesus. Not in too much of a hurry, I hope, to get to the Promised Land. Harriet befriended by Canadian woman who works in nuclear industry and gives her chewing gum. Feelings about nuclear waste and gum fairly similar but smile in a parody of gratitude as Harriet lines up dollops on my thigh.

La Rotovata marvellous. No Brits. No tourism. Shady squares, seventeenth century houses, and further up hill, not sure exactly where yet because lost, – the Embroidery School. Sun burns down and Harriet folds up. *I want a drink now. Drink now! No bars or cafés here, darling, let's walk a bit further up the hill. Carry! Carry! Tired! Ache all over!* Disregarding satirical glances from natives, lug her uphill to what I hope will be a café. No! It is a bookshop. Er – lovely. They will have a map. – *Habla Ingles? No. Français? Italiano? Deutsch? Latin? No, no.* Combination of youthful beauty and sullen unhelpfulness particularly enraging. Stomp out, cursing in Ancient Greek, and feel once more I have been educated to no avail.

Sun smites brow on exit, and first fangs of migraine begin to bite. Pill necessary – but how? *Drink now!* Toil uphill, in heat, desperate for bar, but nothing in sight except beautiful bloody seventeenth century houses. If only other Brits around. The Fat lady, I'm sure, would sort us out in a – wait! There's a Bar! Dark, and Men Only. Ask tremulously for Coca Cola – only international language. Wonder what Erasmus would have made of it. Swallow pill whilst men watch in silence. Harriet finishes bottle and we slink out, sure that Purification Rites will follow our departure.

Terrible hunger. But no restaurants. Only ironmongers and haberdashers. Onward and upward under boiling sun. Harriet weighing thirteen stone at least and emitting death rattle. Stroke imminent – when suddenly, in most wonderful old house ever – Embroidery School. Not sure that I like embroidery much. Dazzling indigenous craft, or meaningless intricacy for enslavement of women? Buy several handkerchiefs that no-one will ever use, dive into taxi, and request bus station.

In taxi reflect that a passion for architecture, like most civilised tastes, inappropriate in a mother of small children. Also wonder why, periodically, one thinks one needs a holiday, and wantonly departs from home, where food, drink, lavatories, shade, and Help with Children are already laid on. Lean back and close eyes against Sun, The Emperor.

ten

CRAWL BACK FROM HOL. to find Spouse very chipper after his idyll in charming secluded corner of seventeenth century. Children fling themselves on him as if returned from a Gulag and not a week in Tenerife with maternal parent, bidet and balcony at their mercy. Collapse in chair and demand cup of Earl Grey. Spouse regrets it ran out on Tuesday and offers British Workmen's tea instead. Reflect how soon men left alone descend to barbarism. Spouse says I look surprisingly pale. Wonder if a new pair of glasses would revive my marriage.

Phone rings. Person called Sally with girlish voice asks for Spouse by Christian name. He says he will take it in his study as children are being deafening. Shoo them into garden but too late. Name *Sally* disturbing. *Of all the girls who tra-la-la, There's none like pretty Sally*. Ransack memory in vain for Sally with face like horse and breath like old tomcat. All Sallys fresh and engaging. Sour feeling spreads through innards. Brick red tea or green eyed monster?

Children burst into kitchen sniggering unpleasantly. Harriet exhibits earthy knickers and admits she sat down inadvertently on crocus bed. Children continue tiresomely hysterical on subject of muddy bottoms. Escape upstairs in search of clean knickers. Airing cupboard just outside Spouse's door. Spouse still on phone. *Yes we must . . . Oh, don't worry about that.* Notice airing cupboard needs tidying. *I'll ring as soon as I can fix something up, then . . . Right.' Bye, Mips.*

MIPS? A pet name – already? Most Intensely Pulchritudinous Seductress? Idea of Spouse fixing something up unnervingly energetic. Hear him emerging, and dive into airing cupboard to avoid implications of espionage. Crack head on boiler and gasp. Spouse surveys scene and demands explanation. Declare that exposure to British climate, after subtropical Canaries, profoundly traumatic and that I must be incubated like ailing chick. 'Certified, more like,' retorts Spouse in a tone of voice he did not use for Sally.

Escorted into garden to witness disastrous mildness of season. Spouse indignantly points out that Greenhouse Effect has brought the Prunus and wild damson into blossom. Irises and croci also rampant. Try hard to be appalled at the sight, but secretly convinced that Greenhouse Effect is what British climate has always needed.

Spouse remarks that by the time Harriet is forty, the only place in the Northern Hemisphere fit for the cultivation of grain will be Siberia. Am so aghast at the idea of Harriet's being forty, have no terror to spare for any other ecological disaster. Mind's eye offers glimpse of Harriet as matriarch, visiting me in my bedsit at the Toynbee Sunset Home. She demands sweeties and when refused, rips out my hearing aid and jumps on it.

Detect assumption that I will be widowed, and question it, especially in view of Spouse's evident rude health and unnatural glow. If he survives me, will he re-marry someone younger and prettier? Cannot help noticing that increasing choice is available in above category.

Alice rings to boast about trip to Bogota. Mention Sally syndrome with what I hope is amused throw-away laugh. Alice recalls that old mutual friend Emma always fancied Spouse and says he looks like Michael Buerk. Race upstairs for Nine O'Clock News. Hypnotised by the way Buerk's lips revolve clockwise, and by the immense burden of compassion in his eyes. By 9.08 p.m. I am deeply in love with him and only wish Spouse resembled him more, especially round the eyes.

After the news, open window and smell night air. Delicious. Positively spring-like. Heart beats faster. Fear sap is rising all over Northern Hemisphere, so fast it will drown us all.

Harriet wakes up crying and says she dreamed she peed in the teapot. Comfort her with thought that it could have been

8 HUIT
EUR 70 B
FR 85 B
US/UK 38 B

much worse. Proud of her ability to have Joycean dreams. Re-read first few pages of Ulysses . . . *warm sunshine merrying over the sea.* Desire to go to Dublin, preferably with Michael Buerk, but doubt whether it would revive my marriage. Sigh, close window, and decide on a new pair of glasses instead. Hoping for Benazir Bhutto effect, but suspect I lack the aristocratic bone structure.

Observe Spouse sleeping and console myself with the reflection that though the similarity to Michael Buerk only fitful, at least no resemblance whatever to Martyn Lewis.

eleven

Peveril St. Canonicorum raised his cold grey eyes from the Baume de Venise. 'An excellent Soufflé Depardieu, my dear. But just one thing – are there no walnuts this year?' Charlotte arose and in a trice her exquisite little Rive Gauche slippers were tip-toeing through the turnips to the rude sod hut where, at this hour, Cherbagov would be at his simple peasant meal. Timidly she knocked and peered within. He was sitting abstracted at the table, his goat's cheese and black bread untouched before him. He saw her, and a look of terrible significance flashed between them. 'Have you . . . any nuts?' stammered Charlotte, a girlish blush mantling her –

Interrupted at this point by phone call from optician to say new glasses are ready. Drive straight there, desperate to see whether pale green frames and amber tinted lenses will bestow air of glamorous Italian psychiatrist, and save my marriage. Probably too late though. The mysterious Sally has rung again, and Spouse is pretending not to notice that I haven't asked who she is . . . I think.

Arrive home in amber miasma and ask children how I look. Henry says. 'Not too fat really. Except from the neck down.'

Harriet declares that if he ever says that again she will kill him. How? asks Henry. 'I will give you a doughnut,' she warns, 'only it will really be a stone.'

Somehow this reminds me there is nothing for supper. Run to kitchen and open fridge. Assailed by remnant of ancient Camembert. Strong cheese Spouse's only apparent vice – till now. Hesitate. Attempt to shrug off Listeria Hysteria, but in vain. Throw cheese in bin, but notice ten minutes later that its signals have strengthened.

Retrieve cheese from bin, throw down lavatory, and flush decisively. Cheese pops up again with insouciant air. Flush again but cheese persists. Wonder how mass-murderers manage with whole bodies. Attempt to poke Camembert out of sight round S-bend with loo brush, but it makes a cheeky comeback from The Beyond. Sure this kind of thing never happens to the Queen.

Using old tablespoon, hoick cheese out onto saucer and am carrying it outdoors when intercepted by Spouse. Declares nothing whatever the matter with unpasteurised products and demonstrates his machismo by swallowing it whole before I can say a word. Asks where supper is, I say On the Way, hoping it will not be his last.

Nothing in fridge except two withered carrots, bag of sprouts dating from eighteenth century, and a couple of half-finished jars of mould. Remember Spouse's opinion of tinned food, and panic. Fly to my shelf of carefully labelled and aesthetically pleasing nuts and grains. Find that pine nuts, pumpkin seeds, sesame seeds and wheatgerm are all rancid and walnuts have gone bitter, unlike Cherbagov's which are poised at a moment of consummate ripeness. Am baffled by the thought of what to do with buckwheat. Feel sure landscape gardener would create chi-chi woodland path with it.

Wonder if Spouse is going to be taken ill, and if so, how soon he could conveniently manage it. Confess that the cupboard is bare. Spouse looks up from *The Independent* and cheerfully suggests that he could fetch some fish and chips. On way out he gives me brief pat on the back, the sort of salutation one might bestow on favourite, but not terribly fragrant, old dog. Children help me to lay the table, horribly excited by idea of chips in a bag. Mind whirls with suspicion. Why Spouse so keen to nip out to chip shop? Flying visit to the mysterious Sally, perhaps? Try to recall features of chip-shop proprietress but sure she is more of a Val.

Spouse returns promptly. Evidently conquered urge to dally with Sally. Children devour chips, remove cod from its batter and eat the batter. Too tired to care. Greasy newspaper still crumpled up on table: not the sort of thing Glenys Kinnock would allow, I'm sure. Catch sight of crumpled newsprint photo of Gorbo with discarded chip on his head. Disturbing image. Feel I have somehow besmirched an icon. Bundle newspaper into bin.

Spouse gives me a strange look. Is this . . . the beginning of the saving of the marriage? I hesitate by the rubbish bin, encouraged by the thought that I am only too fat from the neck down.

'Those glasses are a big mistake,' he says. 'They make you look like an Italian psychiatrist.'

Feel overpowering urge to get back to the rude sod hut.

twelve

HARRIET'S FOURTH BIRTHDAY LOOMS. Spouse regrets he will be away at Conference in York. No previous mention of it. Suspect Northern assignation with the mysterious Sally, who rang again yesterday. Try to shrug off martyred air as know it is unbecoming. Arrange to hire Bouncy Castle for party, to provide children with maximum exhilaration: infantile equivalent of having an affair.

Spouse packs new aftershave: West Indian Limes. Receive, as goodbye kiss, a peck on each cheek. Suppose Spouse is getting into Continental state of mind. Fear conjunction of Sally and medieval alley will, to a man of historical sensibilities, prove fatal. Cannot even console myself with fantasies of Gorbachev as have to organise party. Dread that separate elements of party will fly apart leading to chaos and confusion. State of mind probably similar to Gorbo's, come to think of it.

Henry asks if Julian can come as he does not want to be surrounded by stupid little girls. Reflect that the determined feminism of Henry's early education (Winifred the Pooh, Michaela the Mouse) has not borne fruit. Do not like sound of Henry and Julian – literally or metaphorically. Too much like gay couple. Although why not? Would rather end up as Queen Mother than Ma-in-Law. Could lead to lots of Art Deco and music festivals. Remember Aldeburgh. Alas – suspect Henry's hostility to little girls infallible sign of heterosexuality.

Recruit Mrs Body to keep Henry and Harriet down to a low simmer whilst I rush to shops. Buy eight pencils, rubbers, notepads, and wooden badges for take-home bags. Then remember ten children will be coming, not eight. Stagger back up hill and buy two more of everything. At least have avoided plastic – apart from bags. Have brainstorm and buy ten plastic trumpets. Know, even when paying, how deeply I shall regret it.

Great day dawns with children leaping into my bed and demanding the Bouncy Castle now. Explain it is folded up in garage and must first be inflated. Harriet looks worried. Confides that balloon pump is broken but you can blow the Bouncy Castle up yourself with your mouth can't you Mummy? This thought cheers me up at various points through the day.

Collect cake: wondrous creation upon which four sugar teddy bears have established Gay music festival. Cake says HAPPY BIRTHDAY HARRIOT but do not complain about spelling as feel it might sound like graduate condescension. Buy salt-free crisps, Hula Hoops, cheese and Smarties, and hope that no child will actually die of heart disease on the premises.

Mrs Body provides frightful quivering white blancmange which painfully reminds me of certain parts of my own body.

Reveal cake with panache. 'They've spelt my name wrong!' roars Harriet. Ah well. Time she learnt that education leads irrevocably to indignation.

Children arrive – most of them called Emily – seize trumpets and blow. Cracks appear in walls, skull, etc. Distract with tea. They devour crisps and Hula Hoops but ignore forlorn pieces of apple, tomato, cucumber – monuments to foolish liberal hope. Blancmange shudders and is devoured. 'Poor Blancmange!' says Harriet.

Time for cake. Cannot find matches to light candles. Children seize trumpets again to pass time.

Think how agreeable would be the echoing stillness of York Minster, with only a lover's breath in your ear, and two hearts beating frenziedly through winter coats. Find matches in lavatory where suspect Henry has been conducting environment-hostile experiments with methane.

Light candles. Sing. Harriet blows, coughs, and spits in smallest Emily's eye. Smallest Emily cries for next ten minutes. Try to distract with offer of cake, but Julian objects that cake must be taken home in bags Not Eaten Now. Henry glares. Feel have committed dreadful social gaffe and defer to Julian's *savoir-faire* as he is destined for Eton.

After tea, Bouncy Castle astounding success. Feel many international problems could be eased by access to one. Should have invited Ayatollahs. At last children depart and Harriet bursts into tears declaring that Party has Died.

Spouse rings from York to say it is damned cold, and he's got a frightful sore throat. Go to sleep slightly comforted. Unless of course he's lying.

thirteen

HARRIET MUCH OBSESSED BY DEATH, now she is four. Reluctant to let me occupy lavatory alone in case I expire within. Spouse returns from weekend in York without betraying whether it was Conference or dalliance with mysterious Sally. Declares he has the flu and retires to bed.

Feel cheated somehow. Surely, as I held fort for whole weekend, nay organised and endured children's party in his absence, if anyone's entitled to a bout of flu it is I. Notice that flu has not taken away his appetite. Run upstairs with endless trays. Spouse confides boring symptoms in tragic voice. Harriet enquires if Daddy is going to die. Reply I'm afraid not.

Harriet screams in rage and threatens to kill me with a piece of brown paper. Suggest she tries again after two more days of Daddy's flu by which time I shall be a pushover. Harriet looks puzzled and withdraws to watch *Monty Python* video with Henry. Henry fascinated by, and endlessly replays, animation sequence which includes decapitation. Reflect that *Monty Python* can only be enjoyed fullbloodedly by the childless. Once a parent, strange fumes of disapproval arise from huge toxic dump of unsuspected reactionary sentiments, thinly covered by inch of liberal topsoil.

Detect presence of purple passage and run to study to offload it into novel.

Where was heroine Charlotte Beaminster? Ah yes. In Cherbagov's sod hut in corner of kitchen garden, enquiring about availability of nuts. Cherbagov rises. His brown eyes kindle, swim and brim. No, wait. Optic overload here. Perhaps they just kindle. It is Charlotte's senses which swim. Cherbagov welcomes her to his rude edifice, offers her his arm and suggests a walk to the nut-grove. Charlotte lays her lilywhite hand on the rough linen of his Slavic shirt, and feels beneath it the proud swelling of his *Supinator Longus*. (Charlotte is studying anatomy in secret.)

They have got no further than the rhubarb when Charlotte is hailed by a hysterical housemaid. The Master has fallen downstairs and probably broken his arm. Typical act of self-dramatisation, thinks Charlotte. Cherbagov brilliantly sets the broken bone with sticks from nearby ash tree. Charlotte watches listlessly, feeling anatomy not so very interesting after all.

'Cherbagov!' gasps Peveril. 'You are a stout fellow. I shall not sack you after all. Help me to my chaise longue and tell me your quaint peasant story.'

Charlotte points out that Cherbagov was accompanying her to the nut-grove, but Peveril suggests she can go with hysterical housemaid instead.

Interrupted – not without relief, for novel proving even more frustrating than everyday life – by bell, above. Spouse thinks he can manage two rounds of egg sandwiches and a cup of cocoa. Whilst two eggs boiling, wonder what is the point of husbands when they are not actually putting up shelves or frightening children? Eggs rattle irritably together in seething saucepan. Symbol perhaps of matrimony. Am not surprised, on lifting them out, to find they are both badly cracked.

Phone rings. 'Hello!' says breathless, charming voice. 'It's Sally!'

Heart leaps at the thought that this is the voice at which Spouse's heart leaps – perhaps. Was she in York? Are they in love? What's going on? Inform her that Spouse is laid up with flu, and whilst she is sympathising, search for irresistibly assertive way of seizing initiative and revealing truth.

'I'm doing Population Growth and Religious Dissent with him,' she says, 'and Leonard and I have been saying for ages that you must both come to dinner when you're next in town.'

'Er – thanks.'

She rings off having promised to fix something up.

Not reassured by Leonard. Cuckoldy name. And do not like the thought of her doing Population Growth with Spouse. Horribly aware that truth is still veiled. Wonder if I need assertiveness training. Think probably I do. Perhaps. Must ask Spouse.

Carry egg sandwiches upstairs and brace myself to mention, in casual throw-away style, Sally's call. Spouse is asleep. Sit on stairs and eat egg sandwiches myself. Wonder if I will fancy Leonard. Spouse suddenly appears on landing and says,

'Any sign of those egg sandwiches?'

Go downstairs and boil two more eggs.

fourteen

CONFRONT SPOUSE. 'A woman called Sally rang and said we must have dinner with them next time we're in London.'

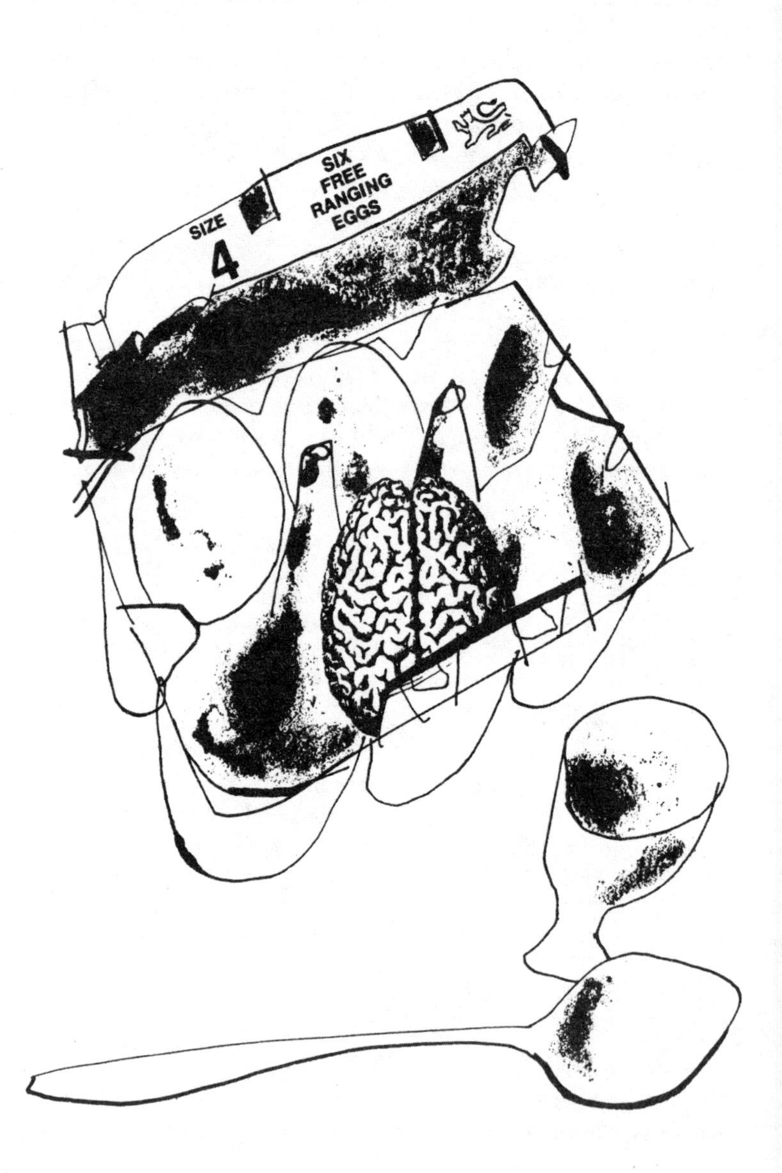
SIZE
4
SIX
FREE
RANGING
EGGS

Spouse turns pale, runs into bathroom and is sick. Not sure if this is symbolic or intestinal. Wonder what to do. Hover outside door. Men never at their best when ill. Indignation at treachery of body, plus morbid fascination with details. Women of course shrug off malaises with weary resignation and boredom. Except Aunt Deborah, perhaps.

Children join me on landing. Spouse emerges, white but dignified.

'Were you sick, Daddy?' asks Harriet.

'What colour was it?' enquires Henry.

Spouse announces, with awful significance of Shakespearian messenger, that his flu has Gone Gastric, and withdraws into bedroom. No mention of Sally.

Henry entertains Harriet till bedtime with deplorable puppet-show: The Old Teddy Bear Being Sick into a bowl of hyacinths.

Watch nine o'clock news in peace. Poor dear Michael Buerk still slightly damaged after interview with PM. Appears to have red bruise on cheek. Closer inspection reveals it is a smear of tomato paste on TV screen. Remember now that Spouse hurled piece of pizza at it on hearing words, 'We are a grandmother.'

Suspect country close to civil war. *La Belle Dame Sans Merci* and her Ironclads versus the Green King and Sir Michael de Buerque. Wish had oak tree in which to secrete fugitive prince. Fear he would not be adequately protected by our small clump of daffodils.

Next morning dominated by coil change. Enter examination room hoping not to fart at critical moment. Take off lower garments and assume foetal position on bed. GP in foul temper at Govt. plans for NHS. Glad that in event of civil war, doctors will be on our side. Speculum inserted. Begin to feel like trussed chicken waiting helplessly for stuffing. Stare at wall and try to converse intelligently about professional ethics.

Old coil removed with mortal twang. Wish urgently for out-of-the-body, or failing that, out-of-the-surgery experience. Tempted to suggest new coil can wait until next week, but know it would provoke lecture about dire risk of pregnancy, and that hollow laugh will not be adequate defence.

New coil inserted. Recall Edward II disembowelled at Berkeley Castle. Ears sizzle: wall wobbles. Doctor still deploring HMG. Clearly wishes he could change their coils to a man. Advises me to get dressed slowly or I might feel a bit squiffy, and departs. Glad to be left alone to die. Close eyes.

Ten minutes later have still not died, so get dressed. Wonder archly if new coil will ever be called upon to do its stuff. Halfway through right leg of tights, feel squiffy and put head between knees. View not exhilarating. Knees used to be best feature once, but now their glory hath passed away. Blame the Government's ruthless pursuit of economic growth. Wonder if Iron Lady has ever felt squiffy after gynaecological attentions. Suspect she consults metallurgist.

Outside, am coaxed onto scales and informed that even without boots, am one and a half stones overweight. Make feeble allusions to frantic lifestyle, which doctor receives with sceptical smile. Wonder when he last had a decent night's sleep – or is that just junior housemen? At doctor's advice, sit in waiting room for twenty minutes before driving home. Read magazines of which Spouse would disapprove. Best moment of day.

Arrive home to find Spouse's appetite returned, but glands up. Requests toast and Marmite with Lapsang. Have to wash up first as entire stock of crockery dirty. Blame Government. Halfway through washing-up, am felled by abdominal cramps. Lie on sofa groaning loudly. Sure glands, however far up, cannot compete with cramps.

Henry says, 'Hey if mummy and daddy both die we'd be orphans! And we could go and live by ourselves in a cave and catch pirates!' Children offer to bring me glass of water. Am halfway through fifth sip when I realise it originated in washing-up bowl.

Spouse appears in doorway, in dressing gown and muffler.

'I've changed my mind about the Lapsang,' he announces. 'Make it Earl Grey. And by the way, that Sally woman is a right royal pain in the arse.'

fifteen

SPOUSE RECOVERED FROM FLU. Great relief. Not at his best when transfixed with self-pity. Sweeps aside suggestion we should dine with mysterious Sally. Dismisses her as most tiresome and incompetent co-editor ever. Feel he is unlikely to be in love with her, therefore. Inexplicably disappointed.

Publisher rings with sickening unexpectedness and alleges that I had promised to send first 20,000 words of Bonkbuster by now to see if it is on right lines. Rashly promise to do so by Tuesday. Horribly aware that after 15,000 words, heroine's bodice still unripped. Not sure I am cut out to be romantic novelist. Characters strangely reluctant to misbehave. Should have been social worker.

Henry runs in and asks if he can go and see *Roger Rabbit* with Julian. Know there are no rear seatbelts in Julian's Father's filthy old Volvo. Have hallucination of dear little Henry flung through windscreen. On other hand, cannot face thought of spending day in dear little Henry's company myself. Weakly say Yes, and offer urgent prayer to St Christopher, though vaguely aware he has gone the way of Peter Walker and Norman St John Stevas.

Lie down on sofa. Disappointment at Spouse's failure to be in love, despair at publisher's ultimatum, and dread at Henry's impending accident, seem to have affected my legs. Do not like Easter either. Baby Jesus in manger ideal family entertainment, but sin and death too much like everyday life. Allergic to chocolate, and chicks and daffodils somehow too yellow. Eyeballs ache.

Harriet appears and offers me an Almond Whirl, at which I realise I have flu and crawl into bed, transfixed with self-pity.

Spouse puts head round door and deduces with sigh that I must've got it now. His flu was tragic blow, mine somehow a moral weakness. His turn to be proud and healthy. Feel I may have underestimated its charms. Spouse offers transistor radio, like doctor in India engaged in sterilisation programme.

Best thing about being ill is listening to World Service. Sure

God listens. Perhaps even runs it. Oh no, wait–John Tusa. All best men bald and dynamic like Gorbo. Am reminded of Cherbagov, virile gardener in Bonkbuster, and writhe with guilt. Wonder if publisher ever asks for advances back, and whether they would accept six months' washing-up in lieu.

Radio 4 very comforting. Aural equivalent of porridge and hot-water bottles.

Listen to Natural History Programme from Bristol. '*We want to find out what happens to the larvae after they drop off the gills of the brown trout.*' Marvel at range of human curiosity. Having the flu rather a larval activity, but fear I shall not hatch into a Princess of Wales or Selina Scott.

Envy life of brown trout. No deadlines, no seatbelts, no marital uncertainty. A few larvae on the gills perhaps, but what of that? Drift off down river of sleep.

Have outrageously erotic dream, directed by Ken Russell, about Gorbachev and self in circus ring, performing bareback. Awake whinnying. Body's lewd inclinations strangely ill-timed. Perhaps as organism sinks towards extinction, it marshalls one last reproductive urge.

Call for paper and pen and feverishly transform details of rude dream into pulp fiction. Not terribly taxing exercise under normal circumstances, but sure temperature is over 100°. Fall back exhausted into light doze, where I am tortured by Nigel Lawson wearing a leotard and black mask.

Awoken by Harriet saying, 'I won't let you die, Mummy. If you die I'll pull you up again.' Not sure if entirely grateful. Bad enough being woken up let alone pulled peremptorily from nice warm death like organic carrot from mulched bed. Realise for the first time the heroism involved in The Resurrection, particularly of The Body. Try hard to open eyes but fear industrial crane may be necessary.

Spouse is sitting on bed reading my recent effusions with a strange smile on his face.

'This stuff is absolutely filthy,' quoth he. 'What a way to earn your living.'

All the same, new light of respect in his eyes. Wonder if marriage will be saved in the end by his Taking an Interest in My Work.

sixteen

ALICE RINGS and enquires How's Life? Unwisely confide details of recent difficulties. Alice explodes.

'Stop behaving like a doormat! Get a dishwasher, fill it up, and then go and get sterilised.' Have Puritan suspicion of dishwasher, and painfully associate idea of sterilisation with boiling water and tongs, but know she is right about doormat. 'Saskia and I have got a flat near the Sorbonne for April,' she continues. 'Drop everything and come.'

Afterwards, scratch head dreamily and whisper, like opalescent rosary, names of Metro lines: *Chatelet . . . Etoile . . . Clignancourt.* Endure intense *frisson* of longing. Wonder if Frenchwoman would experience similar thrill at sound of Morden, Uxbridge, and Cockfosters. April in Paris! Pourquar par?

Dress up as Captain Scott and venture out to inspect garden. Peony Liberation Front raising their red fists, and I can see we are going to have border troubles again. Romans apparently introduced Ground Elder. Another of their unfortunate errors of taste, along with saunas, straight roads and Caligula. Spouse peers at lawn, declares it infested with moss, and blames mild winter.

Indoors, my Daturas have been colonised by microscopic creatures resembling grains of cayenne pepper. Wash them with solution of Ecover. Dilemma: is environment-friendly washing-up liquid toxic enough to bugger bugs? And second dilemma: sneaking pity for pests. Harriet runs in and asks what is the EEC because Daddy is angry with it. Tell her I've never been really sure. Feel EEC needs spring clean even more than my Daturas, and not convinced that Ecover equal to either task.

Henry comes in and asks me what is the difference between a bogey and a Brussels Sprout. Forbid him to reveal it, and suggest to Spouse that children might be conveyed to Mrs Body's whilst we get to grips with various toxic substances. Mrs Body happy to oblige. Children ecstatic at thought of

Battenburg cake and videos. Spouse says he will borrow Mr Body's scarifier and give lawn a thorough going-over.

Brief visit to study, but cannot get absorbed in work.

Distracted by the problem of Yeltsin: excitingly radical and more hair than Gorbo. Also perturbed by need, whilst children are away, to announce authoritatively to Spouse forthcoming trip to Paris. Only inconvenience of trip to Paris, endless uncertainty as to gender of things. No problem for Alice and Saskia, I suppose: everything *La*.

Spouse returns with scarifier and bag of horticultural poison adorned with idyllic rural scene. Informs me that Mrs Body says there are head lice going around. Try not to panic. Hope Henry and Harriet get them so I can demonstrate civilised indifference. Speculate about treatment. Vision of Henry and Harriet with shaved heads. Or am I thinking of something else? Eel-worm? Scrapie? Scratch head. Scratch head again. Cannot remember how often head itches normally. Panic. All right for children to have head lice, but definitely not *Moi*.

Wonder how French treat visiting Brits with nits. Boiling water and tongs? Scarifier? Guillotine? Must tell Spouse I am going to Paris. Go out to garden where scarifier, like lawnmower with frenzied metal comb, is doing its stuff.

'The great thing about moving and scarifying now,' shouts Spouse above din, 'is that it chops up the baby slugs at the same time.' Feel ill and go in again. Try to remember that baby slugs grow up to be adult slugs with horrible orange undercarriages. Recall reading somewhere about biological control. Introduce right predator, sit back and relax whilst it devours pest. Wonder if method applicable to head lice, and if so, which predator appropriate. Would helpful robin on head increase local rumours of eccentricity?

Resolve I shall never disturb fragile eco-balance with chemicals whilst nature provides own solutions. Cheered by this thought, think I will finish off apple pie, but horrors! – silver fish runs out from under crust. Lose rag. Hurl pie in bin. Squirt toxic cloud over Daturas, drive off to buy anti-nit shampoo, and upon return announce firmly I AM GOING TO PARIS IN MID-APRIL. Look of furious displeasure and outrage passes over Spouse's face, but he conquers it.

'Good idea,' he says. 'In fact I might join you.'

Changes his tune, however, at the thought of staying with Alice and Saskia.

seventeen

RARE MOMENT OF PEACE IN LAVATORY. Count blessings: not constipated, Easter hols over, going to Paris next weekend, Spouse not a violent man, etc. On the other hand, why bidet still not plumbed in after three and a half years? And why, in cruel April sunlight, does face increasingly resemble Rembrandt self-portrait? Old Masters inspiring in art gallery: irritating in bathroom mirror.

In study, attempt to increase bonk-quotient in novel. Heroine has succumbed, in sod hut, to Cherbagov's manly urgency. Now it is time for the Assignation in the Plantation. Describe varied native broadleaf trees (subliminal educational pressure: hope publisher does not notice.) Then suddenly think: *where is passport*?

Run to filing cabinet and look under P. Find only old copy of *Vogue*, empty crisp packet and Personal Letters file. Start re-reading them. One and a half hours later, remember passport. Look under D for Documents. Find old pregnancy record-card. Pregnancy and puerperium both described as *uneventful*. Fear this may be posterity's verdict on my life as a whole. Remember Harriet's natal period as a series of blood-curdling crises, but suppose medical profession knows best.

Nothing to eat in house. Drive to health food shop for take-away. On noticeboard see attractive small ad for Anarchist/Buddhist Plumbing Collective. Wonder if they could fix bidet. Anarchist bidet might be exciting. In fact, might be too exciting. But surely Buddhist bidet could lead directly to beatific smile and buoyant sense of Oneness with the Flux.

Buy Mixed Veg Crumble for £1.75. Rather small between four, but OK eked out with potatoes and besides, I must lose weight. Uneasily aware that I could have made twice the quantity for half the price at home, had I been a Buddhist. Decide I am Anarchist instead, and cheer up. Sounds quite sexy. Also intellectually respectable. Next time Spouse criticises domestic disorder (eg watering can, card index, dirty coffee cup and banana skin all in laundry basket), shall say I am an Anarchist.

Children reject Mixed Veg Crumble saying it has a farty smell. Spouse also transparently not attracted to it. Pang of fellow-feeling with Crumble. Find ancient sausages lying in snow at bottom of fridge – like food depot waiting for intrepid British explorer. Throw sausages into hot frying pan and retire immediately. Resulting pyrotechnics resemble Trident trials, but much more dangerous.

Spouse and children devour sausages leaving entire Veg Crumble to me. Eat it all up to avoid waste, and then realise I could have saved second half for supper. Stomach outraged, reminds me of countless promises never to over-eat again. Would never have happened had I been a Buddhist.

Ask Spouse, with devious casualness, if he knows where passport is. Replies *In my desk drawer*. Find three old passports there but none valid. Scrutinise my first one at age eighteen. Though nowadays resemble Rembrandt, at least have outgrown stage of earnest young sheep with twinset and pearls. Extend search for passport to entire house. Detained in attic for two and a half hours reading Spouse's old love letters. Would do him good to see them again. After all, he is a historian.

Without passport, will miss Paris. Panic, and throw watering can, index cards, etc, round room. Wonder how so many Anarchists managed to get to Paris in the past.

Offer children Mystery Prize if they find passport. Harriet instantly retrieves it from dolls' house where it was, appropriately enough, serving as dollies' magic carpet. Inspect it. Henry has added luxuriant nineteenth century moustache to my photo. Wonder if it matters, and think probably not.

Harriet seizes knees and demands Mystery Prize so recklessly promised. After moment's severe crisis of imagination, offer her my lipstick. Shall need a new one for Paris anyway.

Called something like *L'Affaire* or *Boulevard*. Harriet runs off with lipstick unsheathed. Luckily everything in house already disfigured. Glad Spouse did not notice this little episode, though. He was absorbed in my moustachioed passport.

'It makes you look like Balzac,' he remarks. 'Shame you don't write like him.'

Wonder if, in Paris, I might Find Myself, and if so, whether I shall recognise her.

eighteen

PARIS! *Dulcie dans le Metro*. Aims of trip: to avoid having wallet stolen like last two times, and to enjoy brief, and preferably cordial, *entente* with Gerard Depardieu. Arrive at Gard du Nord and hesitate by incomprehensible ticket machines. Ruthless looking man snatches my purse and hisses in French, 'You must put it between your legs!' Close eyes and think of England. Open them to find he has bought me a ticket and is zipping purse back into my handbag.'

Grabs my arm and steers me off masterfully through throng. Am too old for White Slave Trade, so probably destined for *Cuisine Minceur*. He thrusts me through Metro gates and vanishes without a smile. Belatedly realise he was Guardian Angel, and didn't even thank him. *La Belle Dame Sans Merci*. Feel chastened, and keep everything of value firmly between legs till I get to Alice and Saskia's.

Flat an absolute pit. Bidet not working here either: full of old paperbacks. Saskia says I must see Important New Buildings whilst in Paris. Rather dashed by this as had intended to dawdle in Tuileries, Galeries Lafayette, etc. However set off obediently next morning for *Cité des Sciences et de l 'Industrie*. Try hard to like it but lapse into longing for *Place des Vosges*. Good toy shop, though. Buy Henry inflatable globe so he can blow up the world in the safety of his own bedroom. Buy Harriet incandescent dinosaur.

In bar, share table with small hairy man who reveals he is Anarchist. Delighted. Tell him I am too. We agree (in French) that Property is Theft, etc. Offers to show me The Flashing Ball. Do not like the sound of this but too polite to say Non.

Escorts me to back of building where admire huge globe made of mirrors. Anarchist says I have wonderful eyes. Wish he was more like Depardieu – as, I expect, does he. Invent engagement elsewhere. Anarchist accompanies me to Metro saying I am adorable. Tighten lips as know this is expression which Spouse finds most repellent. Finally persuade him to leave by mentioning big Tunisian husband waiting for me at Stalingrad. Embraces me flamboyantly and departs.

Ten minutes later notice that wallet has gone. Flooded with sudden tide of bile against Gallic nation. Recall series of discomforts inflicted by them on us in the past, from Hastings to Twickenham. Not forgetting Racine at 'A' level. Metro worse than hell. Resort of thieves and rogues. Called RATP and in places smells like it.

Attempt to report loss of wallet to police. No Madame, unless you have lost official documents, we cannot report it. My hundred quid not significant. Gallic shrugs. Implication It's Only Money. Must admit, have never been thoroughly persuaded that it *is* only money. Bet they wouldn't think so if it was their wallets that had been nicked.

Try two more police stations, in vain. French policemen beginning to look like ferrets. Imply I should have been more careful and kept bag firmly between legs. Could not close the bag properly because of incandescent dinosaur, but lack the vocabulary to say so. Aware of how much happiness *chez nous* is attributable to effortless access to vocabulary.

Return to flat and recover over Earl Grey. Whole episode sickening. Bloody Anarchists. If property is theft, does that mean theft isn't? Alice distracts me with *Paris Match* containing articles about *Anne: La Princesse Scandaleuse*. Revile French gutter press, then read it avidly. Relief all round that at last she appears to have done the decent thing. Alice remarks that Capt. Phillips is rather like Spouse without the PhD. A frightening thought.

Wonder how Spouse is getting on struggling alone with

children. Feel brief pang of guilt and ring up to say *Ça Va*. Harriet answers the phone and says cheerfully,

'O hello Mummy. There's a nice lady here called Sally and she's been giving us sweeties, you don't mind do you?'

What! The mysterious Sally! Handing out forbidden fruit behind my back? Spouse explains they are sorting out the index to their collaborative book. Sounds bored. But recall from own experience Spouse's ability to sound bored in almost any situation including ones of turbulent passion. Ring off feeling somewhat *bouleversé*.

Suspect I have offended Aphrodite at some point in the past. Tempted to go out and look for Depardieu, but decide on early night instead. Dream I am in rural Hereford, buying Barbour with Fay Weldon, and awake weeping tears of sentimental homesickness.

nineteen

HOVERCRAFT FLUBBERS TO A HALT on Dover beach and am reminded of dear Matthew Arnold's *melancholy long withdrawing roar*, rather like Hovercraft being switched off. Arnold obviously disappointed by France, and not terribly reassured by grimy white cliffs on his return. Wait on Platform Four for boat train to Victoria which seems to have disappeared *down the vast edges drear/ And naked shingles of the world*.

British Rail apologises, several times, for absence of train, and swears blind one will arrive in five minutes. Twenty minutes later, still no train and BR too embarrassed to make further reference to it. Eventually train arrives, BR apologises but hope it will not spoil our enjoyment of the journey. German teenagers laugh incredulously and we all pile in.

Claim corner seat opposite windswept woman even older than myself (increasingly rare species these days: always obscurely grateful to them.) Settle down with Elizabeth von Arnim's *Love*. Train remains rooted to Dover. Brain, ever assiduous to while away time, offers quotations about Dover Beach from *King Lear*. Tell brain Down, Sit, Quiet! but fear series of brain-handling lessons at night school long overdue. British Rail apologises for later departure of this train due to passengers being held up in Customs. Rail under breath at British Rail.

Train departs, forty minutes late, conveys us to field outside Dover, and stops with every sign of finality. German teenagers becoming a little over-satirical. Tempted to Mention War but refrain. Instead smile with mature resignation at woman opposite. Her answering smile oddly radiant. Wonder if she is quite all there. Then suddenly notice that she is holding hands secretly under mac with loose-limbed youth next to her. British Rail apologises for delay due to trains stopped at red lights ahead. Evidently wish us to count our blessings.

Woman opposite exchanges amused glance with loose-limbed youth, who bends down and kisses her gently on ear. Rummage in bag, find old cough-sweet, but cannot dispel bitter taste of uncontrollable jealousy. Return to E. von Arnim and to my dismay discover similar ecstatic relationship unfolding. Wonder if my fixation on Gorbachev has blinded me to the possibilities of chaps with less power and more hair.

Attempt to recall loose-limbed youths of my acquaintance, but can only think of the paper boy. Not sure he is ready for a liaison dangereuse. Can imagine Spouse's reaction:

'Hey! Look! Someone's written *See you down the Rec. tonight Mrs Domum* all over *The Independent*. Can't spell Domum, either.' Pretend to fall asleep, but under lashes watch couple opposite passing notes to each other. Things too terribly sweet to utter aloud. Tear of self-pity gathers in appropriate duct. Inform it it is not needed. Train moves off and BR draws our attention to this triumph. Couple opposite doze touchingly against each other. Evidently exhausted, and no mystery why.

At Victoria, pretend have lost wallet during journey. Tired, kind policeman records entire event in laborious capital letters. Tempted to offer to wield pencil myself but refrain. At least can make insurance claim now, although in train from

Paddington read small print of policy and discover that claims for Cash Lost are limited to virtually nothing, the first £25 of which in any case . . . etc etc.

Curse Insurance Companies, Multinationals, and Middle-Aged Anarchist who nicked my wallet. Feel sense of claustrophobia, immured on overcrowded planet with nothing better than Homo Sapiens for company. Seek comfort in cup of tea. Attempt to flick teabag out elegantly into lid. Most of tea goes with it, but still enough to scald tongue. Wipe table with paper napkin. Too much sugar, silly little perforated plastic stick for spoon. Close eyes and remember days of toasted teacakes 'neath silver salvers. Days when loose-limbed youths were Older Men. Also forced to read Matthew Arnold in those days but can't have everything.

Youth sits down opposite but has acne and picks nose. On arrival at Rusbridge, Henry hurls himself into my arms yelling, 'Where's my present?' Useful preparation for affair with younger man? I wonder.

twenty

AWOKEN AT 2 A.M. BY HARRIET shouting, 'Mummee! My nose is bollocked!' Spouse simulates sleep, and in a pathetic attempt to trump him, I simulate death. Two cries later, however, it is I who fling winding sheet aside and slouch like some rough beast towards the bathroom cabinet.

Recall reading somewhere that Yeats was a virgin till he was forty. Appalling. Though becoming one after forty is no joke either. Attempt to get to grips with the idea of Harriet's nose. *Sinex* (nasal equivalent of Dyno-Rod) is not for children under six or persons of a nervous disposition. Three half empty pots of *Vic* all dried out and long past their smear-by date. Pick nose. Realise this is Appropriate Technology, and go and pick Harriet's.

Almost asleep again when puzzled by vague uncertainty as

to whether we have had Easter yet. Become wide awake with effort of remembering that yes, we have had Easter, and it was awful. Worried about brain. Fear it, too may be bollocked.

On radio next morning, Ministerial Person dismisses CND as 'lunatic fringe'. Explains that though extant weaponry able to kill population of world seventeen times over, necessary to modernise in order to re-kill population another six times in chic new ways. Tempted to stab radio with breadknife, but would only demonstrate lunatic response to rational and sane defence policy.

Plumber (summoned by Spouse) arrives to deliver quote for plumbing-in bidet. Reviles antiquity of bidet and can't do anything for three weeks, love, as have Big Job On. Also can't trust that Gorbachev, love, nuke the lot I say, nuke bleedin' Gadaffi an' all. Departs with paeon of praise to St Margaret. Spouse says plumbing arrangements now up to me as he wouldn't be seen dead on a bidet anyway.

Ring Buddhist/Anarchist plumbing collective and am promised Tom by mid-afternoon. Retire to study and contemplate first 30,000 words of Bonkbuster. Only point in its favour: half an inch thick. Only three and a half inches to go. Sigh deeply. Fear onset of writer's block. Gaze out of window and observe nettles two feet high where should have planted seed potatoes by now.

Spend most of day avoiding Bonkbuster by filling in form for competition. Required to match series of smart polyester non-crease, non-iron dresses with most suitable social occasions: business lunch, dinner with husband's boss, cocktails with clients. Cocktails with clients . . . the very vocabulary enough to drive one to solitary life of oatmeal and water in remote Hebridean cave. Although nowadays most Hebridean caves probably missile silos or toxic waste dumps.

Feel depressed. Pre-menstrual tension? Consult calendar, and discover that PMT should have given way days ago to full-blooded murderous rancour. Perturbed. Feel there is enough on my plate without having to deal with Second Coming.

Doorbell rings. Annunciation? Tall young man with gold-rimmed glasses, wild curly hair, grin like blowtorch and plumber's bag. Tom. Lead him upstairs and hope he is an Ankles Man since that's all there is, these days.

Tom admires elderly bidet, says he prefers them old. More of a challenge. More character. He will get to grips with it now, no problem. Then looks straight into my eyes and asks if it's the same Dulcie Domum who wrote *Charley the Chickpea* and if so, can he kiss my feet now as it will save time later.

Spouse puts his head round door and enquires if it isn't time I collected the children from school. Say *No, I'm busy: you go.* Spouse flabbergasted, and meekly obeys. Perhaps Ministerial Person on radio was right about negotiating from strength.

Sit down on edge of bath. Front door slams behind Spouse, and echoes excitingly in empty house. Silent but deafening crack of breaking ice as spring floods surge down through parched valleys. Purple passage begs to be released but inform it that this time it's life, not art.

Tom kneels before me and gets out his tools. Long, strong, *intelligent* hands. Feel I may be teetering on verge of *Vita Nova.* Is reign of Mars giving way to rise of Venus? Wish I had washed my hair.

twenty-one

OBLIGING YOUNG PLUMBER HAS GONE. At his magic touch the bidet has awoken from its sleep of ages and now flushes hot and cold, as indeed do I, in memory of his visit. Tom. Perfect Old English name. Lovely springy curls (could not help noticing as he grovelled at my feet, fiddling with the lucky old copper piping). Admired my children's books, which he reads to his nephew. Also liked my Portuguese tile – something nobody else has ever even noticed.

Sacra conversazione in bathroom interrupted by Henry who burst in yelling, 'I want a poo now quick! It's looking out of my bottom!'

Reluctant goodbye on doorstep. Tom offers to come round

immediately if ever I have any trouble, but fear it would only lead to worse trouble still. Besides, no prospect of burst pipe for months; perhaps, with Greenhouse Effect, never again.

Furtively kick radiators hoping to dislodge something vital, and encourage children to thrust Play-Doh down all the plugholes, but in vain. Plumbing functions serenely for the first time ever.

Spouse snorts contemptuously at Tom's *Anarchist/Buddhist Plumbing Collective* bill. 'I see the Buddhism is extra,' he observes acidly. Wonder if this is Spouse's habitual misanthropy or something more interesting.

Listen to Schubert's *String Quintet.* Tears of vague longing pour down cheeks. Henry comes in and says. 'Switch off that stupid music, Mummy, I want *Roland Rat.*'

Feel Henry is becoming a barbarian. Can see him heading straight for *Vorsprung Durch Technik.* As for Harriet: my entire educational strategy has collapsed. Maternal insistence on Girls are Best, plus relentless exposure to 100% handcrafted traditional fairy tales, has given her Princess complex. Yearns for silky hair a yard long, bri-nylon tutu and kitsch Prince in lurex tights.

Have definitely failed as Mother, Wife, and Gardener. (Seed potatoes still shrivelling patiently in their string bag.) Also as best-selling writer. Publisher's advance long gone. Warned Spouse about this yesterday and he made dark noises about my having to take on a bit of 'A' level coaching again. Wonder if Tom the Plumber has, or would like, 'A' level Eng. Lit. Probably has it already, but could do different Board.

Mind you, literature dangerous thing. Attribute all my problems to having been presented with *Madame Bovary, Le Rouge et le Noir,* and *Anna Karenina* in first term at Newnham. Conclusion: only possible destinies for married woman: adultery or drudgery. Have failed as drudge too: once more cupboard is bare. Put on extremely ancient lentils to boil.

Sound of letters cascading into hall reminds me that I have also failed *vis-à-vis* the Inland Revenue, Electricity Board, etc. Observe large spiders' webs festooning front door. Perhaps could get house designated Nature Reserve.

Distracted by phone. Mysterious Sally. Declares she was

devastated to find me absent in Paris when she came to work with Spouse on index for their book. Hopes I was having a Naughty Time. Silly cow. Wonder if this is because she was also having Naughty Time. Think perhaps not. Suspect Spouse on the whole too lazy for adulterous passion. Sally insists we dine with them in Dulwich when next in town. Promise listlessly to do so, curiously aware that somehow have become bored with Sally.

Notice postcard lying on floor with other post. Beautiful italic handwriting. Unfamiliar. Try to read signature upside down: MOT? Wait! . . . Tom! Vital organs convulsed with strange and silly spasm. Seize card with trembling fingers. Sally still bleating down phone but have gone deaf. Can only hear card: *Could I nip round one day and get your books signed for my nephew? Tom.* Followed by private phone number.

Most exquisite postcard ever, of course: Durer drawing of primroses. Heart throbs like billy-oh. Tell myself I am a matron and should cease this foolishness. Call Spouse, leave Sally, still talking, on hall table and smuggle my treasure into study. Read postcard forty-six times and seems more wonderful each time. Lift receiver and am poised to dial private number when Harriet runs in and says, 'Mummy! Come quick! It's boiling over!'

twenty-two

DOWN, WANTONS, DOWN. Put tantalising young plumber's postcard in drawer and shut firmly. He wants to come round and get book autographed – at time convenient to me. Not first time I have received such a request from person of opposite sex. Nothing remarkable about it. Will probably slip my mind till end of next week. Got the whole thing in proportion, now. PMT to blame. Have often noticed how it puts the whore back into hormones.

Issue in new era of matronly responsibility by blowing dust

off cookery book and making *Pollo Cacciatore*. Realise it is months since I made anything that aspired to a name. As usual bored by cookery book as no real characters in it – though intrigued by idea of Charlotte Russe. Better name for heroine than Charlotte Beaminster. Wonder if I shall ever manage to get to grips with gelatine before I die.

Spouse and children arrive, lured by scent of real food. 'Ugh not Italian muck!' shouts Henry. Spouse peers incredulously into casserole and asks what I am feeling guilty about.

Quickly confess that seed potatoes still unplanted. Spouse suggests soothingly that perhaps a local lad can be persuaded to do it. Do not wish to examine concept of local lad too closely as fear it may be unsettling. Suspect I may be succumbing to A.E. Housman syndrome: young male beauty Wrekin havoc with middle-aged literati.

Spouse offers weekend in London soon if we can get rid of the children somehow. Tortured by brief vision of young plumber dropping in whilst we are away. Banish vision and accept Spouse's offer gratefully, but fear it may not be enough to keep me on the path of matronly responsibility.

Announce establishment of compost heap and place bucket by sink for peelings, etc. Harriet asks why. Explain concept of Biodegradable, and tell her that we are all, too. Harriet bursts into tears, seizes my thigh and forbids me to biograde before bedtime. Alas – fear I have already broken down into fine tilth. Co-op carrier bags will inherit the earth.

Sit down to unusually good dinner. Halfway through *Pollo Cacciatore*, recall that I have not thought about young plumber for an hour and a half. Congratulate myself. Then lose appetite. Move bits of *Pollo Cacciatore* about on plate. Seems to be more now that when I started. Spouse notices and says if I don't want it he'll have it, and what's wrong with me anyway? Confess to feeling a little sick. Henry says, 'Are you going to actually be sick, Mummy? Great! Can we come and watch?'

Doorbell rings, at which cold nuclear fusion takes place in ribcage. Catapulted from chair by conviction it is Young Plumber. On way to front door notice hands look old. Dart into Futility Room where moisturiser, along with bird's nest

ORGANIC STANDARD
SOIL ASSOCIATION

and old cuckoo clock, repose in laundry basket. Squeeze tube. Enormous custard yellow dollop of moisturiser leaps into palm with disgusting noise. Enough to relieve dessicated elephant. Run to door wringing hands noisily.

Seize doorknob, but slips through fingers. Cannot get purchase. Belatedly realise that key to human happiness is appropriate level of lubrication. Recall shrieking hinges, parties at which wine has run out, etc. Doorbell rings again, but doorknob still elusive. Cry out, 'Just a minute – I'm having a bit of trouble with the door!' with what I hope is musical and lighthearted elan.

Wipe hands on skirt – a moment's desperation resulting in expenditure of £2.50 at dry cleaners – and have cornered doorknob when phone rings. Call out 'You answer it!' hoping it will preoccupy Spouse whilst I have magic moment on doorstep with Young Plumber. Fling door open and bestow smile of radiant delight on Mrs Twill selling flags in aid of starving millions. Try to sustain expression of intense delight and hope it is not inappropriate.

Return forlornly to kitchen. Spouse is picking teeth and looking as if he expects a pudding. Offer choc ices, received by children with rapture and by Spouse with resignation. 'Oh, by the way,' says Spouse, 'That plumber Johnnie rang to ask if he'd left his spanner here. Doesn't know his arse from his elbow.'

Refrain from comment, but set myself simple task till bedtime: confine my thoughts to plumber's elbow.

twenty-three

Charlotte Beaminster walked into the plantation. Blindly, quiveringly, following her —

'Mummeeee! Can I have some crisps?'

'No! It's nearly lunchtime!'

Following her . . . er . . . no, wait, – *the cruel thorns pierced her thin kid slippers but she was impelled towards* –

'Snot fair! I hate you!' SLAM!

the leafy dell where she glimpsed Cherbagov's broad back. He was planting.

Oh hell! *Planting!* The seed potatoes! Burst from study like bat out of hell, seize spade and thrash nettles therewith. Then dig. Stung several times before conquering lazy urge to do without gardening gloves. Go to garage and find pile of gloves, originally pairs, but now promiscuously entangled in commune. Thrust fingers into one and encounter something tickly and alive. Scream and run away into house.

Encounter Spouse and Harriet looking bad-tempered and hungry. Have oft wished at such times they lived in a pit and I could throw them a bun or two at feeding time. Spouse enquires what I was thinking of for lunch. Diverted at idea I should think of lunch at all, and run upstairs to loo. Pursued by Harriet saying she wants a pee too she wants a pee first. Just manage to shut door in her face, at which she roars a threat to pee on carpet. Realise with sinking feeling that I have cystitis.

Another of Aphrodite's jokes. Repentance without pleasure. Have not had cystitis since honeymoon. Remember Siena – just. Harriet goes quiet on landing and I realise she is ransacking my handbag, which I know is full of toxic waste. Place head between knees and wish I was in the Campo, the Duomo . . . indeed anywhere except 196 Cranford Gardens, Rusbridge.

Emerge and rescue bag from Harriet, or Harriet from bag. Brace myself, peer within and behold old matchbox containing two applecores (saved for compost heap); sheaf of evangelical literature I was too polite to refuse in the street, and increasingly dog-eared passport. All liberally scattered with aspirins as 'childproof' lid has evidently come off bottle.

Go downstairs and inform spouse I have cystitis and must go to the doctor. Spouse expects it's that bloody bidet. Seems to have taken a violent dislike to it. Even at this moment, manage – heroically – not to think about dashing young plumber.

'What is this tree?' asked Charlotte, running her long white fingers down the rough bark.

'Pinus Sempervirens.' *Cherbagov's deep, masterful tones vibrated in the tiny balls of Charlotte's* Fabergé *earrings, causing them to tinkle.*

'Lets grab some lunch at the pub, then,' says Spouse. Pluck Henry from sofa where he is watching interminable video of cat and mouse decapitating, crucifying and flaying each other. America's idea of Fun for Kids.

At surgery, am unable to provide specimen so take bottle away to fill later. Go to pub and sit in draughty garden because of children. Leave Spouse to order from pretentious menu whilst I dash to loo with bottle. Whilst attempting to secure specimen, experience worst pang yet of penis envy. Also – blind hostility of fate – loo has run out of paper. Personally I would rather have *Papier pour le cul* than *Coq au Vin* any day, but not sure Spouse would agree. Slip bottle into handbag and return to find children devouring *Les Doigts de Poisson avec Haricots de Heinz.*

Toy listlessly with strange pie, into which many disagreeable vegetables and parts of dead body have been persuaded uneasily to co-exist. Wonder if I am really ill. Remember must drink large quantities. Wonder how much Perrier I could take before exploding. *Charlotte Beaminster felt Cherbagov's hot breath on her face* – sod off, Charlotte! You don't know you're born. Hatch devilish plot to give her cystitis in Chapter Sixteen.

Henry suddenly picks nose and eats it. *Morceaux de Nez.* Am in mid-tirade when Harriet upsets whole glass of orange juice over newly ironed dress. Am just thinking *Nothing worse can happen* when, mopping up too enthusiastically, I knock half a pint of Perrier into my own lap.

Delve miserably into handbag for hankie, and am arrested by strangely softened and blurred appearance of passport. Realise with horror that specimen bottle has leaked all over it. Am begging Aphrodite to have mercy when who should walk into pub garden but dashing young plumber, accompanied by young girl of devastating beauty.

twenty-four

'HI THERE, HOW MARVELLOUS,' says dashing young plumber Tom, stumbling upon us eating *en famille* in draughty pub garden. 'Mind if we join you?'

Spouse frowns at intrusion but mollified by beauty of Tom's companion. She appears to be entirely composed of erogenous zones, seamlessly assembled without any intervening marshes or plains. Feel own body would qualify for EEC grant as Less Favoured Area. Must accept that I am unlikely to be nibbled from now on except by flock of rangy mountain sheep.

'This is Candy,' says Tom. Exhibit delight, as – more convincingly – does Spouse. Candy a foolish name. Rots your teeth just to look at her. Can feel arteries silting up also. Harriet stares reverently at Candy's yard-long hair and legs. Comes round and whispers in my ear, 'Mummy is she a Princess?'

'I've been meaning to ring you about signing that book,' I lie in loud public voice. Truth was I rang Tom five times and he was Always Out. 'Drop in any time when you're passing.' Complete this sentence with synthetic leer at Candy. 'And bring Candy if you like.'

'Candy's off to the States on Monday,' says Tom without any apparent anguish.

'Oh how wonderful!' exclaim with feeling. Candy becoming more beautiful by the moment. Would compare favourably with Bellini Madonna.

'What part of the States?' enquires Spouse, rather too urgently. We all wait in suspense for Candy's lips to open. She has not yet uttered speech.

'Oh . . . all over,' she whispers, at which exciting concept I am convinced a palpable frisson runs through entire male company. Even Henry runs off to remote corner of pub garden to search for and kill small forms of life.

Spouse interrogates Candy further on her itinerary, but am

thwarted in attempts to communicate with Tom by insistent demand from bladder that I go to the loo at once.

Make another attempt to collect specimen, and screw on lid afterwards very very tightly indeed. Hold bottle up to light. Lots of energetic little things swimming around in it. Reminds me of Toddlers' afternoon at Rusbridge Swimming Pool. Wonder if they are benign bugs or not, as now I have collected specimen, can take first antibiotic. Am prepared to use Ecover and free-range eggs but draw the line at the anti-antibiotic brigade. Especially with cystitis.

On way back from loo, suddenly bump into Tom in dark side passage.

'Look,' he says in urgent tone I have only recently encountered in my own pulp fiction, 'I need to have a talk. Can you make lunch on Monday at the Pelican? At one?'

'But – won't you want to see Candy off?' I falter.

'Bugger Candy. Stupid bimbo.'

Cannot decide if this unchivalrous, or not. No, wait: can decide, quite easily, in fact.

'Can you make it?' repeats the passionate plumber, seizing my wrist almost roughly. I drop the specimen bottle which shatters on the quaint old flagstones. Tom looks startled and enquires was that my drink. Reply yes, four hours ago.

Tom bursts out laughing and says I am wonderful but he hopes it was not a pregnancy test. Admit to cystitis. Tom lavishes more sympathy on me than have received from whole human race so far, and promises pints and pints of Lemon Barley water at The Pelican on Monday.

Borrow pub's dustpan and cloth and clear up appallingly humiliating mess with effortless cheerfulness while Tom goes off and buys drinks.

Return to table where Tom is entertaining Henry and Harriet by moving his hair about *without touching it*. Have never realised before what a striking accomplishment this is. Spouse deep in monologue with Candy about Chinese restaurants in San Francisco. Tom sends children off to look for caterpillars and gives me a secret look. Have magical sense that heart has somehow flown its cage and gone fluttering off over neighbouring gardens like emigre budgie. Hope it will not get pecked to death by crows.

twenty-five

MONDAY MORNING. Only two hours to go before tryst at The Pelican with dashing young plumber. Wash hair twice to be on safe side. Hesitate over excuse to Spouse. Reluctant to lie, although have lied to him countless times over such things as How Long Have You Had That Dress? Difficulty inserting contact lenses until realise have still got glasses on.

Work out scheme: collect Harriet from playgroup, request Spouse to give her lunch, then whizz off for naughty date. Harriet on Spouse's hands till arrival after lunch of Tracey, at present functioning as mother's help. Cannot understand a word she says – mostly about *Neighbours* – but have to admit I'd be sunk without Trace.

Stick head round Spouse's study door and announce casually that I am Having Lunch With A Friend and can he give Harriet lunch and endure her till Tracey arrives? Spouse tears himself away with difficulty from big mouldy book and says, 'What?' Receives full thrust of message with barely suppressed outrage. Sometimes behaves as if Harriet is nothing to do with him at all, but an irritating friend of mine, visiting.

Hesitate over make-up bag. Men on this subject curiously unpredictable. Spouse reviles make-up on me but has admired women to whom it has been applied with high-pressure industrial spray. As for Tom the Plumber, he is Buddhist/Anarchist so presumably beyond such trivia. Not quite sure I am beyond it, though. Apply timid minimum but cannot get eyes to match. Wipe it all off but eyes still do not match. Mouth does not match, either. Essay seductive smile and discover tealeaf on tooth.

Collect Harriet from playgroup and loose her into Spouse's

study like ferret down hole of distinguished badger. Escape through front door only to encounter fat man in unpleasant suit determined to sell me conservatory. Mr Brian Thomson – *Pleesto Meecho* – just happened to be passing and thought he might have a look at the site. Recall sending for brochure in moment of madness. Tempted to decapitate him but lack means.

Show him back of house and answer series of, in my opinion, intrusive questions about what I intend to do in conservatory. Vow to cultivate pot of basil containing severed head of salesman. Mr Thomson recommends triple polycarbonate for roof as will easily bear weight of man. O happy triple polycarbonate, to bear the weight of Antony. Agree recklessly to finials, brass whatsits, anything to get rid of him. Desperately aware of finger of watch creeping towards 1.15 p.m. Heart already with Tom at The Pelican and rest of body understandably anxious to join it.

Thomson beats slug-like retreat down path. Phone rings inside house. Sudden panic: could be Tom, wondering where I am. Race back up path and burst indoors. Spouse bearing down on phone looks aggrieved and says *Haven't you gone yet*? Grab phone and hear fatal words:

'Mrs Domum? Would you mind coming up to school? Henry's had a little bump on the head. Nothing serious, but we think perhaps he ought to go home for the rest of the day.'

Race to car and drive like thing possessed through Rusbridge. My baby! Felled by cricket ball! Brain damage perhaps, although in Henry's case unlikely. Dart through red light at roadworks and then see strange flashing in rear view mirror. Furies? UFO? No, police car. Draw in to side of road. Whole body shaking with accumulation of disasters. Stern young policeman with moustache peers through window at me.

Apologise, burst into tears and explain that son and heir at death's door. Policeman remarks that others will be, too, if I drive like that, but finally relents. Issues warning and takes name and address. Did not think it could take human being so long to write 196 Cranford Gardens, Rusbridge, but know I should be grateful.

Arrive at school to find Henry perfectly normal and demanding sausage, beans and chips. Matron puzzled but says concussion's a funny thing and he should go home anyway. Perceive hands of sick bay clock standing at 2.10 p.m. and reflect that I'm in the right place for a coronary. Tempted, but depart.

twenty-six

Charlotte Beaminster fled through the night. Brambles caught at her thin muslin shift: the pale poles of birch loomed up at her in the dark: small terrified animals fled from her path. Up ahead, shaded by sighing cedars, stood the sod hut. Charlotte paused, panting at the door. Moonlight raced across her upturned face. She shook a few drops of Givenchy's Homme Sauvage *onto her wildly beating heart; tossed the wayward curls off her gleaming brow, and knocked.*

Wonder if I should go back to 'A' level coaching. Perhaps even 'A' level marking. Remember receiving huge parcels of tormented teenage scribble. Usually made up my mind about quality of candidate after first paragraph. Hope my own readers less impulsive. Fear impulsiveness main flaw in character. No, can think of twenty others. Remorseless self-abasement also flaw. Would not last long in Cabinet. Definitely a Wet.

Transfer purple passage to word processor to see if it looks any better in black and white. Printer strangely faint. Perhaps affected by excitement. Insert fresh ribbon. Printer still faint. In need of head-between-knees treatment but cannot work out where its head is. Put own head between knees hoping for allopathic effect.

Harriet runs in and cries, 'What are you looking at, Mummy?'

'Please Darling I am trying to work.'

'Even Kings and Queens pee and poo don't they?'

'Yes now please go and play and I'll see you at teatime.'

Remember I promised to send Alice and Saskia a copy of Spouse's article in *The Historical Digest.* Switch on photocopier but green light fails to appear. Instead receive red message consisting of pyramid of balls. Wonder what this means. Electronic verdict on literary labours? Conspiracy of machinery? Phone engineer and he promises to come round with Toner. Feel this is definitely what I need.

Phone another engineer – word processor one – and report faintness. He thinks it sounds like my Solenoids. Do not dare to contradict him. Promises to come and tinker with them before nightfall. Express gratitude.

Harriet runs in and says, 'Come quick Mummy it's all over the floor.'

'Yes Darling in a minute.'

Harriet runs out again. Cast dreamy, casual eye over purple passage. Great charm of historical fiction: lack of machinery. Cannot remember why Charlotte has fled to sod hut in middle of night but do not blame her. Suspect she is on verge of spine-shattering moonlit bonk but cannot face it before tea. Spend several minutes biting nails idly and wondering how hairy Gorbachev's chest is.

Harriet runs in again. 'Can I sprinkle talcum powder on it, please Mummy? Will that help?'

'No thank you, Darling.' She runs out again.

Eventually lure of Earl Grey hauls me from brown study. Wonder if Thursday's crumpets have turned to stone yet, but on arrival in kitchen all thoughts of sustenance dispelled by ghastly sight. Kitchen has become lake. Henry sailing boatloads of Lego refugees towards new life in shadow of cooker. Harriet sprinkling talcum powder on water like Ganges funeral rite.

'What the hell is going on?'

'The washing machine had an accident,' says Harriet. 'Like Daniel did at playgroup yesterday.' Demand whereabouts of Tracey, who at three quid an hour should at the very least be dithering ineffectually with dishcloth somewhere within vicinity.

'She's watching *Neighbours*,' Harriet warns me sternly. 'Mummy can I sprinkle some flour on it?'

'No you bloody well can't!' Harriet bursts into tears.

'Don't bloody shout at me, Mummee!'

'Don't say bloody, please, darling!' Seize towels, kneel down and perform first of what will no doubt become routine domestic bailing-out if Greenhouse Effect up to expectations. At least Spouse absent for day in London. Harriet asks at what age she may begin to say *bloody*. Henry says he knows a worse word. Forbid him to repeat it.

Miserable mopping-up concluded with saturation of seven towels and deep sense that technology is having some kind of revenge. Spouse rings to inform of train time. Confide details of flood. Spouse snaps 'Well, don't just moan about it – ring the bloody plumber!'

twenty-seven

THREE HOURS BEFORE I meet Spouse off London train, and he told me himself to Ring Plumber. Dial Anarchist/Buddhist Plumbing Collective with trembling fingers, describe leaking washing machine, and ask for Tom. Girl on switchboard – or possibly Ouija Board – says it is Tom's day off and a bit late anyway but she will try and get through to Hilary. Try to sound grateful.

Return dolefully to kitchen where children are sliding on wet floor. Say 'Stop it or else!' Henry enquires 'Or else what?' Reluctant to mention Spouse as he is never so effective as a deterrent when deployed long-range. Wonder if I should have smacked harder, earlier.

Tracey arrives in kitchen bearing tray with children's cups, etc: ostentatious evidence of labour, though she and I both know she has only appeared because *Neighbours* is over. Cannot understand why I pay a girl to watch *Neighbours*. Payment entirely appropriate, but should be made by TV station, not me.

Sit down at kitchen table and lower head onto arms. Tracey

takes children out into garden. Wonder if this is tact on her part, or a desire to avoid washing-up. Fear I am being invaded by jaundiced misanthropy. Dread arrival of Plumber Hilary as she will not only be Not Tom, but probably insensitively cheerful to boot.

Never liked the name Hilary, even before H. Spurling. Remember story I heard once that Alan Bennett, when asked what he would like for Christmas, replied, 'Hilary Spurling's head on a plate.' Cheer up slightly. Interesting effect of literary anecdote, even if apocryphal: reconciles one to further half-hour of existence.

Tracey comes in again and declares it is time for her to go but do I want her to do the washing-up first? Warble 'Oh, no!' with deep, though unperceived sarcasm, and wave her goodbye.

Henry chases Harriet into the kitchen with large slug. Escape to lavatory.

Three hours till Spouse's return now seems less of an opportunity, more an eternity. Count single blessing: lock on lavatory door holds despite efforts of Henry, Harriet and Slug to penetrate my privacy. Above the screams, rattles and bangs, can clearly hear the asinine bing-bong of the front door bell chimes. Have always hated bing-bongs and when, five years ago, we moved into 196 Cranford Gardens, vowed they would be first thing to go. Fear that one day it will be that sound which sends me over the edge into barking madness.

Henry, Harriet and Slug go to front door and let in Hilary, enormous woman with crew cut and plumber's bag. Hilary, despite name, pleasantly taciturn,. Lifts washing machine effortlessly out of its hole (something Spouse could not do without coronary) and wrestles with its back bits. Harriet whispers into my ear 'Mummy, is she a lady?'

Suggest to Henry that he escorts Slug back into garden but Harriet says no, Slug is called Nigel and he is to be pet for Lego people and she is going to give them a ride on his back right now. Wonder if this is more or less cruel than putting down slug pellets. Must stop doing that, incidentally. Must also learn how to pronounce Ecover.

Return to lavatory and am sinking into Keatsian melan-

choly when doorbell bing-bongs again. Have often suspected front doorbell mechanism intimately related to pressure on lavatory seat. Suspect it will be conservatory salesman, or worse, but drag myself thither and prepare look of frowsy bad temper to deter boarders.

Fling open door with irritable emphasis and behold none other than dazzling Young Plumber, Tom. Mouth falls open, knees knock, ends split audibly, etc: in short, do not present seductive spectacle. Tom apparently oblivious, stares straight into eyes, or perhaps even soul, which at the sight of him palpably unfolds within ribcage and starts to shimmer. Go red. Lose appetite. Feel uncontrollable smile zoom round past ears and wonder if bottom half of face about to fall off.

Tom puts on expression of mock severity and whispers, 'Nobody stands me up and gets away with it.'

Am about to swoon, but prevented by the application of Slug to my naked calf.

twenty-eight

Delight at unexpected appearance on doorstep of dashing Young Plumber, Tom. Only fly in ointment: Henry and Harriet at my side, equally delighted. They urge him to move his hair about without touching it, like last time. Reflect that this ability is one advantage he enjoys over Gorbachev. Another: can be invited in to tea.

Do so, and abandon all thoughts of Gorbo, not without *frisson* of guilt similar to that experienced recently when Not Voting Labour for first time in life. Cannot believe I am only voter actually attracted by Green Party's Defence Policy. Does not go far enough, in fact. Should be even more alternative. Need research into how to repel invaders with wind, water and sun. Examine own feelings about San Tropez and conclude should not be too difficult.

Children run ahead to kitchen, and in shadowy privacy of

hall, Tom touches my elbow. Not, till now, a part of the body I'd particularly noticed – nor used, since the January sales. Elbow glows in the dark. Feel I have underestimated it. Tom whispers, 'I meant to bring that book for you to sign but I forgot,' and gives simper which, in normal circumstances and on another face, might have been mildly irritating. This particular simper, however, steals around my neck like a swathe of silk. Am so unnerved, I knock Spouse's old school photograph off the wall. It does not break: is this symbolic? If so, of what?

'Is he in?' murmurs Tom. Feel this enquiry is faintly indiscreet, and try to subdue surge of delight. Inform him that Spouse is due back from London in two hours. Words *two hours* also possess mysterious resonance of naughtiness. Try not to think of all the things that could happen in two hours, were small children not relentlessly present. Wonder how *Anna Karenina* managed to get herself Vronskied.

Arrive in kitchen where greeted by enormous bum in boilersuit. Female plumber Hilary! Had quite forgotten her existence. She greets Tom with weary indifference (though don't ask me how) and they exchange masonic remarks about washing machine whilst I put kettle on. Wish children and Hilary could be spirited away on magic carpet for couple of hours' fairy tale adventure. In the event, all sit down to Earl Grey and Jaffa Cakes. Cannot face Jaffa Cake for first time in life. Stomach has been replaced by flock of humming birds. Tom eats three Jaffa Cakes, which disappoints me slightly. Henry demands pickle sandwich.

Eventually children go to see Hilary off. Suddenly kitchen horribly quiet. Stare at table to avoid Tom's eyes. Observe small Lego person face down in pool of pickle. Fear that if I look up, shall find myself in similar situation.

'Hey!' says Tom softly. Our eyes meet with deafening crash. Boiling blush unfolds upwards from soles of feet. Children run in demanding Freez-o-Pops.

Stick face in fridge to cool strange burning. Nothing for children's supper. Only small forked carrot already mouldy at top. Wonder if this, too, symbolic. Will Spouse, when he returns, also want food? Whole habit of putting things in mouth and swallowing them extraordinarily bizarre.

Tom gives children model aeroplane to try out in garden and promises to join them in a minute. Continue staring into fridge, terrified by thought of all the things that could happen in a minute. Phone rings. Seize it with strange mixture of hatred and relief. It is Spouse.

'The bloody trains are completely haywire again,' he says. 'I'll stay in London tonight and arrive tomorrow morning on the 10.15.' Replace phone and turn round to find that Tom is suddenly standing so close, can feel his breath on my eyelashes.

'He's staying in London till tomorrow,' observe in breathless squeak. Tom's eyes generating enough energy to fuel national grid. Only fridge stands between self and abyss. Cling to it for dear life. 'Nothing for supper,' I gasp. 'I'm hopeless.'

Children rush in shouting that aeroplane is stuck in tree. Tom goes out to rescue it whilst I plunge head and shoulders into freezer. Find ancient pizza therein. Children rush in shouting 'Mummy! Can Tom put us to bed?' Nod dumbly. Feel faint at the thought of the fifteen hours till Spouse's return, and wonder how long I can decently force children to stay up.

twenty-nine

TOM AGREES TO CHILDREN'S REQUEST to put them to bed. Prowl around downstairs in state of intense agitation. Direct fleeting curse at British Rail for stranding Spouse in London. Cannot understand why present situation – delicious uncertainty plus unparalleled opportunity – should fill me with such dread. Put on kettle – tho' since recent spate of erotic Maxwell House ads, to offer a cup of coffee might well be interpreted as indecent overture.

Settle into washing-up as most anti-erotic occupation available. But when he comes down, what then? No hope of prolonging washing-up beyond midnight, even with series of fanatical rinses. Shall feel strangely naked when rubber gloves and apron removed. Scrub sink, etc, then front of cupboards. Am scrubbing floor when large pair of trainers appear around door. Realise Spouse has not worn trainers for years: since they were called plimsolls. No elasticity in his gait.

'What on earth are you doing?' says Tom, squatting down with amused smile. Cannot provide satisfactory reply. 'Looks like fun,' he observes, and picking up stray sponge, joins in. Have never enjoyed scrubbing floor so much in life. Whilst on all fours by sink, Tom inspects my S-bend and informs me I need prompt attention to avoid serious crisis. Cannot but agree.

Leap up and make coffee. Suggest we take it out into the garden as know that Mr Twill the Old Marrovian next door will be out there, urging on his courgettes. Sit on garden chair leaving wrought iron two-seater, decent interval away, for Tom. He ignores it and throws himself onto grass at my feet. From this position he can peep roguishly up at me without being scrutinised by Mr Twill, who greets me with a 'Good afternoon, young lady!'

Not sure I look so very much like a young lady when seen from below. Fear parts of my neck are taking on a tortoisesque quality. Extend chin in Pre-Raphaelite thrust to minimise crumples. Unfortunately from this position cannot see anything except blighted apple tree. Suddenly notice weatherbeaten body of old rag doll suspended from a branch, like aftermath of savage rural *coup d'etat*.

'Relax!' whispers Tom, and *runs the edge of his right trainer gently down the side of my old sandal*. Sandal has not felt so excited since solidarity visit to Greenham. Am wondering if I dare look him in the eye when Mr Twill leans on fence and observes,

'I'm saving my best one for you this year, Mrs Domum. It's going to be a yard long, I promise you.'

Express gratitude.

Twill then confides his only fear: that damp weather could

make it go soft at the end. Wonder if I was quite right in the head to come out into garden, preferring the certainty of putrefaction to the possibility of seduction. Raindrop hits me on head.

'Ah, it's raining,' observes Tom with scarcely concealed delight, and gets up with decisive upward lunge. Dolphin-like. Wonderful thing, trainers. Or perhaps youth. Wonder how young he is, and hope not uncontrollably so. Follow him up garden path with increasing sense of panic.

Immediately we are inside kitchen, he turns, relieves me of tray, sets it aside, and takes both my hands in his. For a moment, or perhaps several years, we stand transfixed by the sink. From time to time, tap drips with cold and lonely sound. Tom's hands warm and trembling. First time for years I have held hands with another man – not counting the gay curate in 1983. Wonder if kiss coming, and what I should do if so.

'You are so very – ' Tom halfway through tantalising observation when doorbell rings with mad BING BONG and I tear myself away to answer it.

Alice on doorstep with suitcase. 'We're on our way up from Penwhistle Festival,' she says. 'I tried to ring but the phones were all buggered. Saskia's just locking the car.'

Tom appears in hall and says he was just going anyway, only dropped in to see if the kids and I would like to go to Rusbridge Save the Rainforests Day next Saturday in fancy dress. Nod dumbly. Tom departs with chivalrous, though wasted smile to Saskia. Wonder if he will still fancy me when I am dressed as Brazil nut tree attended by Harriet as savage marmoset and Henry as *pistoliero*. We shall see.

thirty

COLLECT SPOUSE FROM STATION IN MORNING. Wonder how tactfully to convey the ghastly news that Alice and Saskia have dropped in on their way up from Penwhistle Festival and are firmly ensconced. Indeed, when I left house, both loos were monopolised. Alice and Saskia past mistresses at joint monopoly. Stereopoly, in fact.

Wonder if Spouse can tell just by looking at me that in his absence I have held hands with another man. Both hands. Have been as it were, ambisextrous. Something wrong with my brain this morning. Overeducation, possibly.

Spouse strides out of station scowling and greets me with brusque enquiry as to whether I have brushed my hair this morning. Admit not. Grasp nettle and explain that Alice and Saskia's arrival has coincided with disappearance of hairbrushes.

'Oh my God!' says Spouse. 'Not those two! Turn round. I'll go back to London.'

Promise soothingly that I heard them say they would depart after lunch. Uneasily aware that this is a lie, and that lunch itself presents massive intellectual challenge as Alice and Saskia are vegans. Or is it vogons?

Spouse announces he will have lunch in his study on a tray. I retort he will do no such thing and remind him how I periodically endure his Great Aunt Elspeth. Spouse falls silent as do I, at this painful reminder that it won't be long till August skies darken at her approach.

Arrive home to find kitchen table strewn with evidence of Alice and Saskia's presence: breakfast debris, shopping, discarded mélange of newspapers, piles of grubby underwear, dog-eared paperbacks and unfolded map of Cornwall.

'God help Cornwall,' observes Spouse, supposing it to be their destination. Explain anew that they are returning therefrom. Spouse expresses sympathy with the public cleansing departments of the peninsula in the wake of A. & S.'s departure. Do not mind their mess, myself. Experience fleeting sense of moral superiority – all too rare in this household.

Alice and Saskia appear, greet Spouse with playful rapture and subversive remarks about The Great Historian. Spouse cringes – a sight worth ten dirty tables. Alice then launches into interminable account of Czech film they have seen at Penwhistle. I go to collect Harriet from playgroup and return to find Spouse still enduring details of Krapzac's camera technique.

Hesitate over putative vegan lunch. Cannot remember whether taramasalata was ever alive. Or do I mean hummus? Academic in any case: only spread available is dregs of Strawberry Jam, suspiciously grey at edges.

Alice persistently enquires whether I can remember *W.R.: Mysteries of the Organism*, and Harriet equally persistently whispers that there is Something Walking About in her Knickers.

Answer Yes, I can remember *W.R.*, though only a very rude bit involving Plaster of Paris. Inspect interior of Harriet's knickers and remove small, and possibly aghast, beetle. Alice enquires if I remember *The Fireman's Ball*. Reply not sure I can remember anybody's. Laughter: on Spouse's part, hollow. Harriet asks Why is everybody laughing? Why why Mummy, why why why?

Suddenly Alice and Saskia announce their intention of going into Rusbridge for lunch. Remember now that when faced with small children they alternately ignore them or flee. Feel sure that a few hours of Henry after school will do the trick.

Spouse so relieved at sudden cessation of Czech cinema talk, does not even complain about tinned tomato soup. Know I must get back into novel and resolve to think hard about heroine Charlotte Beaminster after I have enjoyed little luxury: five mins' reflections on dashing young plumber Tom, and how we stood by the sink holding –

'Oh by the way,' says Spouse, 'I stayed with Sally and Leonard last night. I promised them we'd go up and see them next weekend.'

How can I tell Spouse I already have date: to go with Tom to Rusbridge Save the Rainforests Day disguised as giant Brazil Nut Tree? Tomato soup turns to dust and ashes in my mouth. Not much difference, to be honest.

thirty-one

SPOUSE HAS ORGANISED WEEKEND IN LONDON chez Sally (formerly The Mysterious Sally but now I have mysteries of my own, hers have lost their patina) and her husband Leonard.

Cannot understand why Leopard conjures up images of swiftness and brightness, and Leonard images of geriatric groping. As for Tom – well, as George Eliot understood, the word resonates with perfect manly grace. In fact, when she understandably tired of being a Mary Ann, why did she not become Tom Eliot? Had there been more Tom Eliots, they might have been merrier.

'What about the children?' Spouse provides long-overdue interruption to this mental drivelling. Have brief hallucination that he has demanded divorce whilst I was not listening.

'The children?'

'When we're in London next weekend.'

Hesitate. Time for Last Stand. Over the top.

'I'm afraid there's something I've got to do here next Saturday.'

'What?'

'Rusbridge Rainforests Day of Action.'

Spouse bursts into sardonic laughter at thought of Rusbridge Rainforest, and makes allusions to several species glimpsed in High Street, which, in his opinion, would be better off extinct.

Enquires if I am actually organising it and on discovering I am not, suggests a cheque for £15 would more than compensate for my absence. Feel vaguely hurt. Tempted to offer Spouse cheque in lieu of my company in London.

Sinking feeling reinforced by knowledge that I must ask Mrs Body to entertain Harriet for Saturday night. Harriet will resist savagely as she associates staying there with being properly washed.

Once Spouse is safely in study, tiptoe to phone and write note to Tom on exquisite card (eighteenth-century painting of

strawberries). *Sorry Saturday no good. Have to go to London. Alas! D.D.*

Admire own brevity and restraint for several minutes, but literary satisfaction poor substitute for libidinal sensation. Sigh. Must get back into novel soon as have quite lost thread and long since spent advance.

Post letter on way to collect Harriet from Playgroup, and nerve myself for ordeal of telling her that instead of dressing as marmoset next Saturday, she is to go and be mercilessly scrubbed at Mrs Body's. Harriet screams and says she hates me.

On arrival home Spouse announces, 'That bloody plumber was here again. Said something about the S-bend. I told him there was nothing the matter with it and sent him away with a flea in his ear.'

Heroically hide shame and horror at these words. Wish urgently that I was another form of life. Preferably flea in young plumber's ear. Lost in the warm whorls of flesh. Sucking the sweet juices of life.

'Mummeee! I want an ice lolly!'

'Not before lunch.'

'I hate you!'

Phone rings. Fly to it. Tom, surely: seeking salve for flea. But no. Woman's voice.

'Air hellair Dulcie this is Sally! Something fraightful's happened! Poor Leonard's got shingles! So I'm awfully sorry but Saturday's orf!'

Dear, darling Leonard! How could I have associated him with geriatric groping? Tactful, timely, resourceful Leonard! Swift, bright, feline, dappled Leonard! Uncoiling his magnificent shingles in the tropical sun. Flashing to the rescue through the dark dripping rainforests of marital and social obligation!

Give Harriet ice lolly after all, and fly to word processor to unload what bids fair to be purplest passage in pulp fiction.

'Charlotte Beaminster flew to her escritoire. She seized the pearl-handled pen and a piece of thick creamy paper adorned with the hated crest of the De Las Palmas de Santa Cruz. She wrote madly, the words bursting from the nib in hot, rushed blots: "Yeltsinborg, July

18th: Dearest Cherbagov, drop everything! My husband is called away to St Leonardsburg! I come, I come!"'

But wait: *could* Cherbagov read?

thirty-two

Charlotte Beaminster paced restlessly about her boudoir. In two hours she would make her appearance at the Harvest Home. Already she could hear the whine of old Alexei's fiddle on the night air, and the thump of the goatskin drums echoed the tumult in her heart. What should she wear? Would Cherbagov's rough peasant hands snag her St. Germain satin, or bruise the bodice of her Brussels lace? Thank heavens Peveril had been called away to St Leonardsburg, and her maid Ludmilla had been given leave of absence to tend her mother who was dying of boils in a turf hut in the next parish.

'Mummee! Can I go as a princess?'

'No you can't go as a princess. It's supposed to be a Rainforest Fancy Dress.'

'I hate the rainforests they're stupid!'

'Look, Harriet, I've already explained that if the rainforests are all chopped down there won't be any –'

'I don't care! I want to go as a princess!'

Princess syndrome deeply established despite intensive propaganda about Liberté, Egalité, etc. Harriet runs off to inflict vengeful watering on my pathetic basil seedlings. (Sown three months too late: am fatally out of tune with Dame Nature.) Thought of Dame Nature leads with unpleasant directness to idea of Spouse's Great Aunt Elspeth, poised to swoop down upon us in August. Only consolation: Rusbridge Rainforests Fancy Dress Parade in afternoon, squired by glorious young plumber Tom.

Penetrate attic and wrestle with problem of disguising myself as giant Brazil Nut Tree. Find faded green crêpe paper and attempt to create leafy crown therefrom. Crafts never my strong point. Wonder if I can disguise my torso as a tropical trunk without altogether abandoning all pretensions to feminine outline. Find v. old shapeless brown dress, probably once Aunt Elspeth's, and try it on, complete with leafy crown. Resemble not so much tree as crazed Serbo-Croatian ratcatcher.

Spouse puts head round door and enquires if I have stolen his stapler. Deny all knowledge of it despite uneasy sense of guilt. Stapler symbol of patriarchal marriage; penetrate and transfix. Spouse withdraws without commenting on my attire, despite opportunity for sarcasm. Sometimes his silences even worse than his utterances.

Harriet appears as princess in puce tulle donated by Mrs Body, and glittering wig made of shredded foil. Accept *fait accompli* and if asked, shall say she is an endangered species of tropical bird. Henry announces he wishes to go as an anaconda, at which my last remaining flicker of arty creativity is extinguished with resounding hiss. Suggest he go as a rubber tapper with bucket and large black moustache. Henry rejects bucket and insists on impersonating man-eating form of wild life. No disguise necessary, in fact.

Suggest he could go as Indian covered with brown bootpolish and wearing only small loincloth. Henry seizes bootpolish with joy. Harriet shouts 'Me too!' and throws off her tulle. Struggle ensues, during which kitchen floor is covered with polish, albeit the wrong sort, for the only time in its life.

Hastily burnish children, hoping that Spouse will stay safely in his study. Improvise loincloths from teatowels and shepherd children to car. Leave note: *Gone to Rainforests Fancy Dress Not Sure When Back*. Tempted to flee with darling young plumber Tom to new life in Amazon basin. Or indeed in wash basin. Heart beats fast at thought of him. Rush parking and somehow lift adjacent car briefly into the air with my bumper. Pretend not to notice and hope nobody else did.

As we enter park, large gorilla comes up and carries Harriet off screaming into the throng. Half grateful, half anxious. No doubt glimpse of future son-in-law scenario. Gorilla returns, pulls head off, and reveals itself as Tom.

'You look wonderful,' he says, at which my leafy canopy slowly keels over forwards onto my face. Children spy

Bouncy Castle and run off. Sit on grass all afternoon staring into eyes of adoring gorilla. Recall David Attenborough once enjoyed similar episode. Recklessly promise to go and have tea at Tom's place next week and listen to his Dire Straits albums. Appropriate, somehow. On return to car, discover boot polish all over back seats and stapler, deadly reminder of matrimonial obligations, under banana skin on floor.

thirty-three

'Not here, Cherbagov!' panted Charlotte, as his rough peasant hands fumbled with her tippet. 'In the hayloft! I want you in the hayloft!'

'This is the hayloft, Madam.'

Charlotte wished she had paid more attention to estate management. So this was the hayloft. She had expected it would be more comfortable, somehow. No matter. This was the moment for which she had longed. A whole night with Cherbagov. How opportune that Peveril had been called away to St Leonardsburg!

'Just think, Cherbagov! We can be together until dawn!'

'Well, until three, Madam. I shall have to slip away then to a meeting of the Anatolian People's Liberation Front.'

Charlotte wrinkled her fine, parchment-like brow. Politics! How unfortunate she had taken so little interest in it. Or was it them?

'Couldn't I . . . come with you?'

Cherbagov paused in mid-caress and emitted a short, animal-like laugh.

'Surely you're not in favour of Anatolian Liberation, Madam?'

'Why not? I could open the gardens to the public for you, if you like. We made over 3,000 doshskies last year for the Imperial Limbless ex-Governesses Association.'

'Anatolian Liberation,' explained Cherbagov, gnawing her clavicle, 'would mean the end of this estate. It would be split up and distributed to the proletariat.'

Well, why not, thought Charlotte. She had always found the estate a great bore. And she rather liked the thought of labouring in the fields at Cherbagov's side, dressed in a simple cotton shift edged with broderie anglaise and a naïf motif of rosebuds.

Aroused by this vision, she seized Cherbagov's buttocks. 'Why,' she thought, 'there's more hair on his buttocks than on his head.'

'Let me admire your firm foundations!' she cried impulsively. 'Stand in the moonbeam, you wonderful primitive creature.'

Cherbagov obeyed. The day of the Anatolian Liberation was not yet come. Charlotte gazed in awe at his magnificent fundament. But what was this? On the right cheek was a red mark . . . surely a map! A map of the Yeltsinborg peninsula! What did this mean?

Even as she pondered this enigma, a dreadful sound burst upon the night: the clatter of hooves and wheels. From the hayloft window they saw her husband's personal Porschka roll into the yard. The family crest flashed on the door as he sprang out. For a moment he paused in the moonlight, and Charlotte saw something protruding from his cloak: something long, smooth, highly polished and double-barrelled. Her heart pounded madly as she watched Peveril disappear into the house. In thirty seconds he would find her bed empty – her maid absent – the telltale signs of marital revolution.

'Now, woman,' growled Cherbagov, clasping her conclusively to his hairy side, 'you are truly one of us.'

Charlotte was taken aback. He had called her 'woman'. Was she a woman, then? She supposed she must be. Not that it mattered. At any moment Peveril might burst into the hayloft and blow their brains out. Cherbagov's, anyway. Charlotte feared he might not bother with hers.

'Come, Cherbagov,' she urged. 'Let us enjoy one last embrace ere death claims us.'

But Cherbagov seized her roughly by the wrist and hurried her down the hayloft steps and across the dewy field of swedes, towards the shadowy depths of the Regenwald . . .

Lean back exhausted. As that bloke said on that programme about Elisabeth Frink last week, you lay the table and sometimes the gods come to sup with you. Wonder who he was. Wish I'd seen more than the last five minutes. Elizabeth Frink probably handsomest woman in Western Europe. Wish I'd had bone structure instead of . . . whatever it is. Still, have achieved stunningly thrilling chapter of pulp. Wonder why I have heard no sounds of children for last three hours. Brief spasm of fear, but little likelihood of more than one coma at a time.

Meet Spouse in kitchen and report great progress with Bonkbuster. Spouse doubts whether it could hold a candle to tied Test Match for excitement. Am beginning to feel it is positive duty to have tea with delectable young plumber tomorrow. Have earned it, anyway, after today. Children, accompanied by Tracey, burst in and Harriet enquires urgently if I am going to die soon. Think perhaps not.

thirty-four

TODAY'S THE DAY. Delectable young plumber Tom 'At Home.' Offering tea and Dire Straits, not to mention risk of Dire Consequences. Wonder if I shall manage to –

Dawn thrust its sensitive fingers through the tangled canopy of the Regenwald. Charlotte Beaminster's Rive Gauche *kid slippers were torn to shreds. But still Cherbagov plunged on, deeper into the forest. A tear as sweet and crystalline as a droplet of* Château d'Yquem *fled down Charlotte's cheek.*

They reached a clearing where rude shelters had been improvised from wood and canvas. Some rather hairy peasants were tending a fire, and a girl who looked familiar was carrying a pot of water.

'Ludmilla!' cried Charlotte in amazement. 'I thought you were nursing your mother. You told me she was dying of boils.'

Ludmilla cast down her eyes and trembled.

'I'm sorry Madam – ' she faltered. But Cherbagov broke in.

'This is no longer Madam!' he beamed, slapping Charlotte rather too heartily on the back. 'This is Comrade Madam.'

The peasants gathered round. Some of the older men made convulsive movements towards their forelocks, then thought the better of it.

'Comrade Madam has defied the Count,' Cherbagov went on. 'She has shrugged off the hated yoke of the De Las Palmas de Santa Cruz.' Here several of the men spat – rather unnecessarily, Charlotte

thought. 'And she has joined the A.P.L.F.*!' A ragged cheer went up, and the peasants gathered round, congratulating her. Charlotte felt gratified but somehow in need of solitude. She touched Cherbagov's sleeve.*

'Could we not retire for some hours to one of these rude shelters, beloved?' she murmured. But Cherbagov shook her off.

'Don't call me "beloved",' he growled. 'That is the language of bourgeois socio-familial manipulation. Ludmilla will show you where you may rest. I must attend a meeting of the Manifesto Group.'

Charlotte sighed and obeyed – something for which she had been well trained.

Later, lying on a dirt floor, and covered by a wolf's skin whose original owner, she feared, had not enjoyed perfect health, Charlotte meditated on the sudden change in her fortunes. Soon she would have to pluck up her courage and ask where the bathroom was.

Yet she had gained something indefinable – something, she was sure, that was beyond price. What a shame it was so indefinable. Perhaps Cherbagov would be able to tell her what it was.

'Political credibility!' affirmed Cherbagov some hours later, munching a turnip – with his mouth open, Charlotte could not help noticing. Charlotte was pleased to have achieved political whoss-name. But she could not escape the sense that something else indefinable had been lost. Something to do with her relationship with Cherbagov. On the estate, where it had all been so secret, and he had cloaked his fierce desires beneath a veneer of deference . . . her Fallopian tubes writhed briefly, like a pair of earthworms in the rain, at the memory of such excitement.

'Can we not have an hour or two alone together this afternoon, bel'– Comrade?' she whispered, listlessly watching a Transylvanian swine chewing up one of her discarded slippers. The constant presence of the common people around the fire and in and out of the rude huts was beginning to jar on her nerves. Dear simple folk! Could not they all go off truffle-hunting, or something?

'Life is communal here, Comrade Madam,' grinned Cherbagov, picking his teeth with a birch twig. 'But after the Finance Committee meeting this evening I look forward to creeping under your wolfskin.' Well, that was something. But how could she prepare for a tryst without access to a bidet?

Model 2

BIDET! – Plumber! – Tea! Ten minutes late already! O perverse Muse. Absent for almost a year, then descends at worst possible moment. Race to front door – then through glass spy taxi disgorging unmistakable bulk of Great Aunt Elspeth. Must escape. Must dodge G.A.E. and fly to darling Young Plumber. Flee into back garden and leap over wall into Mr Twill's arms.

'Mrs Domum!' quoth he. 'This is so sudden.'

thirty-five

MOMENT OF SOCIAL UNEASE. Have leapt over garden wall into Mr Twill's marrow bed in order to avoid Great Aunt Elspeth, cruising menacingly up garden path towards front door like U.S. aircraft carrier. Had to escape to achieve tea *chez* darling young plumber Tom – for which already late. Had reckoned however without Mr Twill: delighted by my appearance and intent on showing me his Zucchini.

Explain furtively that escape necessary *vis-à-vis* Great Aunt, who expects Organic Oats, as yet unbought, for breakfast every morning. Must fly to shops or will be in disgrace for years. Amazed at facility with which I lie to Mr Twill, whereas when addressing Spouse most reasonable and transparent remark oft feels like monstrous untruth.

Our front door bell dimly heard venting a muffled *bing bong*. Suspect Spouse also venting muffled monosyllables as appalling Aunt not expected for two days, and he had just settled hock-deep into seventeenth Century sexual mores. Also inevitable irritation: where is Dulcie?

Tip-toeing down Mr Twill's front path, that's where. Decently screened by vast privet hedge. Mr Twill dangerously excited by sense of conspiracy. Squeezes my arm as I slip through gate. Dive into car and pray for starter motor to work. It does, first time. Dart deftly through traffic. Venus with her Winged Boy as outriders perhaps. Not out of wood yet, though. Juno palpably breathing down my neck. Can smell her Yardley's English Lavender Water.

Cannot avoid huge traffic jam in High Street. Roadworks, no doubt to repair damage caused by last roadworks. Stationary for long time behind large van. Juno triumphant. Van bears address of company in 'Royal Berkshire'. How come Berkshire so bloody Royal? And which Royal Berk was it named after?

Suddenly traffic moves, as do heart, liver, etc. Have managed so far not to think too closely of dashing young plumber but body, impatient with brain, demonstrates it can think of him all by itself. Hands tremble on wheel, flock of butterflies seek to escape from ribcage, and foot slips off accelerator. Stall at green light. Maddened toots behind. Juno smiles venomously. Suspect she resembles Great Aunt Elspeth.

Eventually gain Porritt Gardens and park, without style, outside No. 29. Tom lives at No. 44. Do not wish him to see, or hear, me park. Lurch out of car, bang head on doorframe, and whilst reeling, drop car keys down drain. Juno, with horsey laugh, flies off to supervise Meals on Wheels Committee Meeting.

Stare down drain. See only black water. Wish briefly to disappear beneath it forever, till Venus grabs me by scruff of neck and propels me towards No. 44. Car left unlocked, but what the hell. Hope it will be stolen as that would obliterate loss of keys.

Tom opens door looking less than enchanted. No smile. Distinctly feel small hairline cracks travel across heart, like Jerry-built garage. Seek to speak but choke instead.

'I thought you weren't coming,' observes Tom in guarded tone. Apologise, stagger in, collapse in v. old armchair, and confide ghastly details of Great Aunt, Roadworks, Banged Head, Key Down Drain, etc. Suddenly dazzling sunlight seems to flood through room, but it is only Tom's first smile. Provides strong red tea and Brahms' Wind Quintet.

Glance round room and recollect gratefully that young bachelors even more untidy than self. Wonder again just *how* young and hope over thirty. Settle back for Brahms. Tom sitting opposite. Odd: had expected Dire Straits. Soon evident that Tom knows what he is doing, choosing Brahms. Wind Quintet definitely a threat to bourgeois marriage.

Tom's eyes kindle. Distinct danger of spontaneous, simultaneous combustion. After long hot summer the merest spark could lead to disastrous conflagration. Aware that I am prolonging this metaphor to avoid thinking about what will happen next. Observe with relief – and terror – that Tom no longer looks less than enchanted.

'If you're not out of here in two minutes,' he says suddenly, 'I'm coming over to kiss you.'

Limbs twitch convulsively as if to escape, but recall that car keys down drain and escape on foot impracticable as blood has left legs for more interesting arenas. Hope I will not die in next two minutes. Hope also I will not taste too much of P.G. Tips.

thirty-six

TRANSFIXED in Young Plumber's armchair. Awaiting threatened kiss. Not our fault – driven to it by Brahms, and helpless in mesmeric power of Venus and her doves cruising around room and shedding luminous blessings. Tom the Complete Angler: has power to reel my madly thrashing heart up throat as far as tonsils.

Tom suddenly discards his glasses and dives onto his knees before me. 'It's no use,' he says, 'I can't not.' Then I am kissed. Room rocks, etc. Close eyes and hold on tight. Cannot concentrate on kiss, though. Literary training informs me that 'I can't not' is a double negative and therefore undesirable. Wish literary training would wait till consulted and not take initiatives.

Kiss suddenly ends. Open eyes. Tom's eyes, very close, colour of moss. 'God you're wonderful!' he pants. Suddenly become wonderful again for first time in ten years. Top of my head flies off. Hope literary training has gone with it, and good riddance.

Tom, without glasses, reminds me of someone. Another kiss unfolds but cannot concentrate on this one either. Who is it he resembles . . . ? Who . . . ? Ah yes. Pam Shriver. Odd. Small Talk Archive within head enquires if I remember how Pam Shriver did at Wimbledon this year. Inform Small Talk Archive that its grant has been cut and there will be no appeal.

Second kiss ends, and frenzied hug develops, hampered by intrusion of my knees. Tom's heart beats wildly against my kneecaps. Would prefer to be standing up but not sure how to broach the subject, and in any case no air in lungs. Suddenly possibility of standing up pre-empted by Tom who pulls me masterfully down onto hearthrug. Gaze into each other's eyes for 150 years. Tom's breath sweet – unlike hearthrug.

First prone kiss steals upon us. Aware that have not yet uttered protest and feel I must. Keep eyes open as token of resistance. Spy old saucer under chair. Saucer loaded with fag-ends and ring-pull tops from cans. Fleeting desire to leap up and seek vacuum cleaner. Extraordinary: Juno's last stand? Shut eyes and resolve to do better before kiss ends. Am at last loosing moorings and drifting out into dazzling bay when phone rings on floor close to head.

Scream and recoil. 'Ignore it!' commands Tom. 'Answer it!' I insist. Sure it is Spouse, Mother, Primary School Headmistress or scandalised Prime Minister intent on defending family values. Tom argues with phone about his availability to mend burst pipe. Burst pipes in August? Juno more resourceful than I thought. Leap up, collect belongings, hover by door. Venus drooping by waste paper basket: her doves moulting onto carpet.

'I must go!' I insist as he rings off. 'I'll have to run home, because the car keys are down the drain.'

Tom says he will take me – insist he mustn't as his eccentric old van all too recognisable. Will take taxi. Anguished goodbye behind grimy front door.

Run to High Street and scour horizon for taxi. How to explain why car keys down drain in Porritt Gardens of all places? (Residential, secluded, down-at-heel, and never before visited by a Domum.) Start to run home. Brain, so intrusive during amorous play, now refuses to offer ingenious solutions. Hey! Can say car keys fell down drain in High Street! Thanks, brain. But wait! If car keys down drain in High Street, why car parked in Porritt Gardens? Stop, panting with stitch outside video shop, and wish I was any other form of life, preferably hermaphroditic earthworm several feet below ground.

Taxi appears. Leap in and glance at watch. Cannot believe what I see. Strange things happen to time when one is being wonderful. Taxi driver wishes to discuss shortcomings of persons of Middle-Eastern origin. Agree with every unheard word, whilst privately forming plan to ask Spouse for spare car keys and return immediately to Porritt Gardens, *alone*. Lean back and breathe deeply to fend off heart attack. Shall need Personal Assistant to negotiate adultery without mental and physical disintegration. Venus and her doves not enough.

Leave taxi chugging at gate and run indoors. Spouse, already bored to point of homicide, taking tea with Great Aunt Elspeth (waiting in vain for her Organic Oats). Pant out request for spare car keys. Spouse does not move and gives me a strange look.

'Why,' he enquires, 'is there a dog-end in your hair?'

thirty-seven

OUTBURST OF INGENUITY NECESSARY. Spouse and Great Aunt Elspeth staring mystified at my head . . .

'Well, you'd have fag-ends in your hair if you'd been face down in the gutter trying to get the car keys out of a drain!' Spouse grins patronisingly – always a terrifying sight – and rises to his feet.

'Where is the bloody car?' he sighs. 'Where's the drain? I'll have them out in no time.'

Cannot tell him car is in Porritt Gardens, scene of recent

mildly amorous episode on darling Young Plumber's floor (hence fag-end). Porritt Gardens obscure and (except by adulterers) unvisited. Pause to greet Aunt Elspeth with effusiveness and apologise for chaos. Great Aunt Elspeth retorts with mock affection that she expects no less of me and that it is all simply wonderful. Little does she suspect that since being kissed by plumber I am now *really* wonderful. Spouse asks with deadly sympathy why I don't sit down for a nice cup of tea with G.A.E. whilst he, Superman like, Boldly Goes to rescue car, keys, etc. Feel wonderfulness run off me and disappear down cracks in floorboards.

'You can't!' I stutter. 'Because of a secret! To do with your Birthday!'

'But my birthday's not till March,' objects Spouse. Insist that This Particular Secret has to be ordered seven months in advance. Great Aunt Elspeth simpers that it sounds like a premature baby and wouldn't that be a wonderful birthday present.

Make feeble excuse and dash out, promising to collect children from Mrs Body's on way home. Spouse glares, as indeed would anybody faced with another half hour alone with G.A.E. rampant on favourite topic: babies.

Leap into taxi and demand Porritt Gardens. Driver obliges, and resumes rabid racist monologue which is soothing balm after the strain of lying to Spouse and Great Aunt Elspeth. Arrive at Porritt Gardens to find Tom inspecting my car.

'I was just going out,' he beams, 'and paused to caress your bumper, when I noticed you'd got a flat tyre. Shall I change the wheel? Or would you rather do it yourself?'

Sit on pavement in sunshine and admire Tom's back, legs, etc. whilst he does masterful things with jack. Wheel changed, and we bid an excitingly restrained goodbye in street.

'I'm going to Tuscany for two weeks,' says Tom. 'I'll ring you the minute I get back.'

Drive off to Mrs Body's with sick ache in pit of stomach. Do not like Tom's ability to go off to Tuscany without any apparent regret. Rehearse scenario in which Tom tells me he was going to go to Tuscany but can't possibly tear himself

DUNLOP FORT

away from me. This fantasy supposed to be gratifying but makes me feel even sicker.

Detect long-forgotten undesirable side-effects of Being in Love. Attempt to console myself with reflection that It Never Lasts. Self rejects consolation and bursts into tears whilst parking outside Mrs Body's. Blame it on disastrous conjunction of PMT and parking, and blow nose on hem of skirt.

Children grumble on way home about the inadequacies of our video collection compared to Mrs Body's. Distract them with information that Great Aunt Elspeth has arrived, no doubt with tooth-rotting butterscotch and artery-silting shortbread. Children cheer. Hope they will not discuss farting in her presence like last time.

Arrive home to find Great Aunt and Spouse in garden, observing – in Spouse's case, with reluctance – flock of housemartins engaged in aerobatics. Reminds me of poem by G.M.Hopkins but cannot recall details. Recall details and poem is not by Hopkins but Marvell, and not about housemartins but a kingfisher. Great Aunt informs children that every year housemartins go off all the way to Africa.

'What!' exclaims Harriet open-mouthed. '*Walking*?'

Mention flat tyre to spouse, and say I changed wheel.

'All on your own?' he enquires incredulously and I furiously insist yes, on my own, before realising that I could easily have been helped by any passing stranger without adulterous implications. Also realise hands are too clean to have changed tyre, so thrust them deep into pockets where encounter decomposing banana skin retrieved from floor of car.

On way up path, trip and bash nose on concrete. Could not get hands out of pockets fast enough. Feel that were I a housemartin, I would be toddling northwards up the hard shoulder of the M.1. on my innocent way to Africa.

thirty-eight

Great Aunt Elspeth's glands go down, for which we are all very grateful. She joins us once more for breakfast, though lamenting that my oats are not organic and we are therefore ingesting invisible poisons with every mouthful. Forbear to point out that sugar is not terribly good for you either, especially the six ounces a day that she must get through. But the sickening sweetness of her butterscotch and shortbread are nothing compared to the pictures of Alastair's little ones.

An immensely fat and cross-eyed toddler, and a bald and venomous baby faintly resembling Mussolini, are displayed for our admiration. Mussolini is wearing frilly nylon drawers which would, in my opinion, be more appropriately employed as a lampshade in a suburban brothel.

'Deborah has Alastair's nose, I think,' observes G.A. Elspeth. Have already forgotten which child is Deborah, but my memory of Alastair informs me that the important thing is that neither of his daughters should have inherited his brains.

'Hazel is such a lovely little mother,' continues the besotted monologue. 'She makes all their little dresses and things By Hand. Alastair is so very lucky.'

Unlike poor Spouse, landed with a woman who has never made anything by hand, except a mess. A woman who, even at this moment of reverential gazing at photos of G.A.E.'s grandchildren, is hoping fervently never to meet them. And is wondering instead how soon her pliable young plumber will return from Tuscany so she can fly to his arms.

'I think little Gabrielle is going to be a real beauty.' Not sure which child is Gabrielle, but convinced that G.A.E. should, as a matter of urgency, arrange a visit to the optician.

Photos of children succeeded by interminable series of Alastair windsurfing on unpleasantly bleak loch – taken at a distance of several hundred yards without a zoom lens. Suppress shudder at severity of Hibernian landscape. Long for the twinkling humanism of Tuscany, belfries peeping among cypresses, terracotta, grapes, and warm young arm stealing around my waist. Feel that in spirit I have already left Rusbridge and am speeding southwards like heat-seeking missile.

'Mummee! Can I watch *The Sleeping Beauty* video pleeeeese?'

Harriet has already watched it ten times in last few days, but can hardly refuse as it was another of Great Aunt's high-calorie offerings. Also aware that it immobilises Harriet for seventy-two minutes. And though it reinforces her desire to be a 100% nylon princess kissed into life by Prince, a few wise maternal words about the delights of an independent life as female brain-surgeon or plumber will soon redress the balance.

'Where are the men?' enquires Great Aunt. Stifle merriment at this description of Spouse and Henry, and advise her that they are at the Dentist's – an appointment postponed three times already because of Spouse's manly apprehensions of physical pain. Wonder if it would be easier to conduct clandestine affair with dentist than plumber. With plumber one is dependent on caprices of domestic machinery: with dentist one could conduct long course of treatment and return looking orally battered without suspicion.

Great Aunt feels we should watch *The Sleeping Beauty* with Harriet because of the frightening bit, and produces wicked little box of chocolates to fortify ourselves against this ordeal. Prepare to sneer, inwardly at least, but as the Handsome Prince fights his way desperately through the forest of thorns to reach his loved one, feel strange prickling sensation in nose. By the time he has slain the monstrous fire-breathing dragon and turns to gaze longingly at Her Turret against the clouds, floods of tears are streaming down face.

Recall that I have always sat dry-eyed through *The Messiah* but am often moved to tears against my will by cornflake advertisements.

Suspect I have a 100% nylon sensibility. Whip out hankie and murmuring excuse about needing to look at my work for a moment, escape. In hall encounter Spouse and Henry, wearing NO CAVITIES badge, despite Great Aunt's efforts. Spouse sees my tears and makes martyred reference to PMT. Cannot tell him it was Walt Disney.

Escape briefly to study and wonder when My Prince will come.

thirty-nine

Reasons to be cheerful: Great Aunt Elspeth has returned to Fife, school term has started, Worcesters available at greengrocers, and autumn fashions flattering to the Fuller Figure. Nevertheless, cheerfulness elusive. Instead am haunted by sinking feeling, as if breakfast muesli has set like concrete in tum. Young plumber must have returned from Tuscany days ago and has Not Phoned.

'Who the hell is Tom?' snaps Spouse, reading a postcard as he brings in the mail. Heart leaps into mouth and prevents answer. 'It's worse than the bloody Christmas cards. Who *are* all these people?'

Tosses Tuscan postcard onto table, clearly indifferent to any explanation. Just as well, since difficult to account for arrival of holiday postcard from The Plumber. Reach casually for it and knock teacup over. Red Sea engulfs postcard. Rescue and mop with kitchen paper (not recycled: pang of guilt).

Glance casually at card but it was written in real black ink and all that remains, is . . . *frescoes* . . . *magical* . . . *toe*. Admire swirling italic script. Tingle at *magical* and *frescoes* (words that have never passed Spouse's lips so far as I am aware) but worried by *toe*. Anxious lest Tom's nice young toe damaged by collapse of ancient cupola.

Postcard from Siena: one of my favourites. Simone di Martini's *Peace*. Slant-eyed figure reclining on sofa, holding olive branch and clearly not the parent of small children.

Thumps from upstairs where Henry and Harriet are repeatedly jumping off bed. Timidly remind Spouse it is his turn to do school run.

'I took them yesterday!' he retorts with glare.

Dumb at this outrageous lie. Unless it's amnesia caused by

the aluminium saucepans. Rise and grab car keys. After all, might see Tom's battered old van somewhere. Or could even drop a casual postcard in at Porritt Gardens: *For God's sake* RING! – I mean, *Hope holiday delightful. How about drink sometime?*

On way to school Harriet and Henry argue about whether witches are real, because in the Roald Dahl story it says they are. My opinion urgently canvassed, but children irritated by Agnosticism. Cannot get interested in subject of witches, or indeed anything except whether or not it is All Over already, before it has even begun. Invaded by feverish listlessness. On way home irritated by way Roald Dahl always looks like typing error, and is even more unpronouncable than Ecover.

No sign of Tom in town. Perhaps under magical fresco he met dazzling Etruscan nymph and cannot face telling me out of compassion for my extreme middle age. Perhaps he will never ring or write or call again, but let me collapse slowly from centuries of neglect like exhausted old cupola. After parking car examine face in mirror and can clearly see signs of earthquake damage.

Phone fails to ring all day despite my staring at it a lot, and rearranging it several times in attempt to make it more comfortable. Cannot face lunch: Spouse goes alone to Dog and Duck. Hope he meets dazzling Etruscan nymph there. Indeed wish all men would disappear from face of earth. We could grow daughters in cupboard under stairs, like bulbs in bowls of compost. O hell! Bulb-planting season already. Have no desire to see the spring.

But wait! Perhaps young Tom ill. Keatsian expiry in foetid Italian Pensione. Toe apparently marginal, but how fast might fatal case of blood-poisoning swarm up slim young thighs and settle in corrosive flood about heart? Wonder if I should phone Buddhist/Anarchist Plumbing Collective and make discreet enquiry.

Spend an hour which should have been dedicated to work, trying to invent name for Tom's firm. 'Zen and the Art of the Ballcock?' 'The Piping at the Gates of Dawn?' 'Plumb Crazy?' Suggestions on a postcard please. A postcard. The Simone di Martini could mean anything. Could betray intense desire to communicate. Or could be guilty gesture. *I promised you my heart and soul but as it turns out here's a postcard instead.*

Next day in post, envelope addressed to me in swirling italic black ink. Let it lie vibrating by my plate until Spouse has departed on school run, despite assertion that he did it yesterday. Then seize and disembowel envelope. Within small tactful card and single line like Haiku: *Your phone is out of order. Please get it fixed.*

forty

INFORM SPOUSE THAT PHONE IS OUT OF ORDER, and say I will go to public phone box and report it. Spouse observes it can stay broken forever for all he cares. Try to remember when Spouse last made observation that was not sardonic or furious. Leave house tingling in anticipation of ringing Tom and arranging assignation. Pavement mysteriously replaced by trampoline.

However, Mr Twill happens to be passing phone box and urges me to use his phone instead. Decline. Twill persists. Tempted to brain him but new Telecom featherweight receiver unequal to task. Finally whisper, simpering, 'It's like this you see – I'm phoning my secret lover!' Twill departs, winking. Fool!

Dial Tom's number with trembling fingers. He will be out, of course. Heart thrashes about in ribs like agitated cat in basketwork cage waiting to see vet.

'Hello?'

Cat, or possibly heart, has fit. Confide identity. Tom insists I leap into taxi now and storm round to Porritt Gardens as he is absolutely desperate to see me. Persuade him to wait until 7.30 if I can get babysitter, if not, 9.

'Why can't He put them to bed?'

Brief silence. Aware that Spouse has only put children to bed at historic moments, such as Great Aunt Elspeth's urinary crisis at Swindon, or in his moments of acute difficulty with seventeenth century.

'Tell him you've got an evening class. Then you could come every Thursday.'

Intoxicated by thought of coming every Thursday, promise to see him later, and ring off. Am halfway home when recall I have still not reported phone out of order. Turn on heel, not for first time in life.

Three hours later, communication with outside world restored. Immediately ring Alice and confide that I am in the grips of acute adulterous temptation.

'For God's sake Dulcie do the decent thing and cuckold the bastard!' she cries, at which I feel a strange but mercifully brief pang of sympathy for Spouse. 'Any woman with an ounce of spunk in her would've done it years ago!' Feel encouraged, though she rings off lamenting Tom is not a woman.

Spend diverting ten minutes imagining present predicament if Tom was female (played by Pam Shriver) and self, male (played by Paul Newman – no, come off it Dulcie, Denholm Elliott.) Denholm Domum would not give a toss whether Plumber Pam was under thirty or not. Nor would he have to ask Spouse to put children to bed, were Spouse female. Attempt to imagine Spouse as female, but easier to imagine him as Martian.

Enter Spouse's study with placatory cup of coffee. Spouse halfway through Milton on Divorce. Inform him I am attending Life Class this evening. Spouse utters incredulous laugh and enquires Whatever Next? Manage – just – to refrain from telling him, and instead point out that he should put children to bed and Remember their Teeth. Spouse looks weary and agrees with martyred sigh, as if to suggest Milton would never have stood for it.

Worried about transparency of alibi. Phone Tech to see if Evening Classes have actually started, but phone permanently engaged. Then – shock horror – publisher rings out of blue to enquire about progress of Bonkbuster. Inform him I am engaged upon research. Feel guilty that I have not given a thought to Cherbagov, let alone Gorbachev, for a fortnight.

Feel I am becoming not only amoral but apolitical, and irresponsible because I do not care.

Collect children from school and in complete absence of maternal impulse to nourish, offer them Monster Munch Crypto-Crisps, Day-glo Mousses and cans of Silt. Aware – too late – that this will cause maximum hyperactivity at bedtime. Kiss them and depart. Harriet wails that she wants to go to Life Class too but I promise her that her turn will come.

Driving urgently down High Street when souped-up Cortina, overtaking van, roars towards me in head-on posture. Blood runs cold. Realise I am about to die without consummating passion for Tom or finishing sewing on Harriet's name tapes, and whilst driving in opposite direction from Tech. But I suppose death's a bit like that.

forty-one

STEP UNSCATHED FROM PRANG. Relieved that opponents also intact, though satisfied to see that their Cortina has acquired an extra syllable and become concertina. Wonder if brain has been jarred into Crossword Overdrive where it will stick forever. Pat redoutable old Volvo on its mildly-dented snout, and exchange insurance details with Cortinians.

Policeman materialises from nowhere, falls on Cortinians with the Wrath of God, and suggests rather too persistently that I should ring my husband. Ignore this impertinent advice and resume Flight to Eden at 10 mph.

Park erratically in Porritt Gardens and ring Tom's bell with vibrato. At sight of him collapse, shaking, and explain that I owe my life to Swedish Steel. Tom says he does not know which to kiss first, my Volvo or me. At this, burst inexplicably into tears.

Carried upstairs for first time in life (at over forty, which just goes to show). Am laid on large lumpy bed under sloping attic roof, covered tenderly with quilt, stroked, and offered clean hankie to blow nose on. Get giggles, then hiccups. Tom says he will go and make pot of tea and I am Not to Move.

Lie back in strange tingling moment of peace. Admire ceiling. O Attic shape! Items of Tom's clothing flung about as if frozen in mid-dance. Haunted suddenly by Ode on a Grecian Urn. *What socks and shoes are those? What trainers loth?/ What boiler suit which struggles to escape?/What shirts and trousers? What wild ecstasy?* Enjoy being still unravished bride of quietness. Teddy bear waves at me from exploded armchair. Imagine Tom as little boy, and weep anew.

Wonder if I had died in prang, how Tom would have reacted. Imagine funeral in Abbey. Spouse and children in new coats: Aunt Elspeth pale but triumphant: Mrs Body weeping loudly in crackling polyester, and Tracey examining split-ends throughout Runcie's eulogy. Mozart's *Requiem.* Tom absent from ceremony: has committed Hara Kiri under full moon with old piece of lead piping. Spouse eventually remarries vacuous nymphet, realises too late how wonderful I was, and starts deluging heaven with poems, like Hardy.

Tom enters through Pearly Gates bearing steaming tray. Greet him with wan hiccup. Not the seductive soiree one might have hoped. Struggle into sitting posture, ingest tea and doughnut, then have to go to loo. On return, find Tom in bed apparently naked apart from glasses.

'Come here!' he whispers.

Charlotte Beaminster shivered under her wolfskin. She heard a distant howl. Was it a wild dog? A charcoal-burner driven insane by the solitude of his calling? Or her husband hell-bent on revenge and brandishing some recently-sharpened instrument of death? There was a rustle – Charlotte uttered a little shriek – and found herself in Cherbagov's arms.

'Sorry I'm late, Comrade Madam!' he breathed into her hair. 'The Finance Committee always gets bogged down in Any Other Business.' Charlotte turned her tear-streaked face up to his, and his rough peasant kisses blew her ebbing spirits into a blaze. How different was this rude tent from her silken boudoir at Yeltsinborg! No matter if Peveril found them here and she and Cherbagov were hacked to bits by his Myrmidons. This was her destiny – her old nanny might have called it Sin, but she, Charlotte, gave it another name. She felt the

ENGAGED

thrilling pulse of Life itself shooting in her small and exquisitely serpentine veins.

Suddenly 10.30 p.m. Groan at necessity of exchanging hot skin for cold scorn. Allow ourselves another five minutes' gazing. Drink desperately at Tom's eyes like parched old camel preparing for long trek across blinding sands. Both weep foolishly sideways into pillow. Wonder how short-sighted he is and hope my crows' feet are minimised by the tender attic light.

On way home, realise that only woman Spouse resembles is Princess Anne, without the Good Works. Spouse, if Princess, would be President of the Sod the Children Fund. As I park heroic Volvo, anxiety redoubled by the thought of confronting Prince Anne. Spouse looks up from *Newsnight* with regal sneer.

'So,' he says, 'how was your evening of naked flesh?'

Jaw drops and blush right up to ceiling before I realise it is only a reference to Life Class.

forty-two

PEER IN MIRROR FOR SIGNS OF ADULTEROUS GUILT. Astonished to find I look 150 years younger and appear to be emitting a strange glow as if radioactive. Have interminable shouting match with Harriet about which knickers she must wear to school, culminating on her part with,

'I hate you Mummy you horrible load of slug-poo!'

Glance in hall mirror en route for breakfast and already the radiance of secret dalliance has dimmed.

Not that Spouse would notice, immured behind *The Independent*. Henry sulks as both Dinosaur and Outer Space cereals have run out and there is only Weetabix. Harriet shares her toast with My Little Pony (subversive gift from Mrs Body) and Old Rag Doll who looks like Michael Foot. She improvises dialogue between them, thus:

(My Little Pony): 'What's the matter with you this morning?'

(Michael Foot): 'You woke me up in the middle of the night, you bastard!'

Exchange startled look with Spouse as if to imply that This is Something She Must Have Picked up at School. Though we are both familiar with Spouse's ejaculations whilst driving.

Wonder if I shall ever have breakfast with Tom. Imagine morning in Bellagio with bougainvillea etc. Lose my appetite and acquire foolish smile. Spouse enquires what I am smirking at. Pretend it is something Harriet once said. 'What was it I said Mummy what what what?' Unable to recollect anything Harriet has ever said and take refuge in loo. Harriet hammers on door yelling, 'What was it I said Mummy you bleeding bonker!!?'

Suppose there must be worse behaved children in the world but hard to imagine them. Loud report on landing followed by indignant screams suggests Spouse has stirred from his habitual inertia into a timely act of violence. Must be a relief after hours of philosophical speculation. Cannot bring myself to smack children but murkily relieved that Spouse can. Wonder if this relates to unilateralism somehow but unable to pursue this thought as entirely unrelated to breakfast in Bellagio with Tom.

Harriet's screams grow distant, Spouse evidently roused enough to undertake school run without being nagged. Return with relief to bougainvillea.

In privacy of my study, telephone Alice to report amorous success. She is disappointingly off-hand about it and in a fury about something on her annual tax return.

'Just listen to this, Dulcie!' she roars:'*A woman should state after her signature whether she is single, married, widowed, separated, or divorced.* No mention of men having to state anything at all.' Express incredulity and outrage.

'It's so they can decide which of us are just asking to be raped,' Alice insists. Enquire what she stated after her signature and she declares it was LESBIAN THANK GOD. Feel this is not auspicious moment for prolonged rhapsodies about Tom, and ring off.

Must work. Must recover interest in Gorbo but his remarks on Nationalist Movements are not helping. Manage to feel outraged about Estonia for two minutes. Global conscience evidently not entirely submerged beneath Breakfast in Bellagio.

Mail arrives: used to be highlight of day, now tiresome interruption of erotic daydreams. Several letters threatening me with prizes of £100,000 or timeshares in Costa del Sol. Also invitation to Read *The Spectator* free for four weeks. Tempted to Explore the Brothels of Bangkok with A.M.Daniels, but not sure I am up to *The Spectator* at the moment. Instead danger of becoming a Mills and Boonie. Had forgotten how being in love subdues one's intellectual vigour as well as one's global conscience. Love it love it hee hee.

Over coffee Spouse confides deep feelings of self-pity because his sabbatical is over. Blasphemes predictably over need to bomb off down motorway to academe every God-damned day. Refrain from observing that ambulancemen, who contribute more to human welfare in a morning than he will in his whole life, would be glad of a week's sabbatical let alone several months'.

Wave him off with specious expressions of sympathy and return to house which even in normal circumstances would now seem gloriously empty. Not sure if I could go the whole hog with Tom on sacred territory of matrimonial home. Try to feel guilty at this vile thought, but instead burst out singing.

forty-three

SPOUSE OBSERVES FROM BEHIND *The Independent* that a man in Iran has been hanged for adultery. Choke on muesli. Spouse adds that formerly it was only adulterous women who paid the price, usually by stoning, and do I think this represents social progress? Wonder if Spouse means anything by this, and hide face by plunging beneath table on spurious errand to pick something up.

Ghastly sight down there. Four Lego persons covered with tomato sauce, evidently victims of atrocity involving half-eaten sausage and one of Henry's trainers. Take refuge in levity and suggest that if Iranian adultery laws introduced here, would instantly achieve Green Party's population reduction goals, but there would be nobody left to have round to dinner.

Spouse lowers *Independent* and asks if I am implying that most of our friends are adulterous, and if so, can he have details? Take Lego people to sink, ostensibly to wash off tomato sauce but actually to hide face again, and suggest that Spouse's colleague Geoffrey may well be wolf in sheep's clothing. Spouse retorts that no one would ever be tempted to stray with a Geoffrey especially that one. Think perhaps he is right about Geoffrey but that Jeffrey Quite Another Matter.

Henry and Harriet run in accompanied by a deafening noise which, for once, I would willingly have been engulfed by earlier. Restore Lego man's hair onto his head with satisfying snap, then observe that his wife is committing adultery in bottom of sink with Lego ambulanceman. Reflect that you can't trust anyone in this *fin-de-siècle* plastic world.

Wonder what it would be like to be stoned as adulteress, but would prefer Death by Polystyrene.

Make futile attempt to rake Harriet's scalp with fine-toothed comb as recommended in recent letter from school about nits. Feel sure that Harriet's dark thickets conceal not only head lice but several endangered species of small mammal and possibly also barn owl's nest. Perhaps as so much countryside vanishes beneath bulldozer, our children's heads will become only wildlife habitat left.

Spouse concedes he may as well take the children to school en route for the motorway as he has an 'early' lecture (10 a.m.: wonder what ambulancemen would think of this definition of *early*.) Wave goodbye to family with heroically concealed relief.

Mind now free to embrace long-suppressed thought of Tom, which washes up from soles of feet in warm wave of delight. Have installed myself comfortably on loo and am gazing out dewy-eyed at autumnal beauty when phone rings. Run to answer it without bothering to pull knickers all the way up. (How soon, when one is alone in house, do extravagances of etiquette fall away.)

'I'm calling from the corner of the street,' observes phone menacingly. It is Tom – at realisation of which, my tonsils twang. 'I've just seen them drive off,' he continues. 'Is the coast clear? I mean, you haven't got anyone staying with you, have you? Can I come round? It's my day off. If I don't see you within ten minutes I'll explode.'

Insist he comes round immediately to be defused, or least submit himself to controlled detonation.

Eighty-five percent joy at his early morning impetuosity accompanied by fifteen per cent horror that I have not yet had time even to rake my nits. Run to badly-lit hall mirror and observe customary Rembrandt self-portrait, only younger than usual and with manic gleam in its eye. Only have time to slap cheeks, lick lips and anxiously sniff armpits before the sound of trainers pounding up the path requires me to open door and surrender to desperately hot tongue and strong but trembly arms.

Begin to feel faint after about five minutes and realise that I have not breathed since front door closed on our embrace. Fill lungs deeply to prevent coma, and rest head on Tom's chest as so satisfyingly depicted on *Mills and Boon* covers. Then above his thudding heart, hear horrifying sound of male footsteps striding up path, and simultaneously notice Spouse has left his briefcase containing lecture by front door. Footsteps stop. Wait, paralysed, for imperious key in lock, horrible gust of fresh air, and possibly, first stone.

forty-four

WHAT HAVE I BEEN PLAYING AT ALL MY LIFE? Especially in last few months. Moved to these meditations not only by present marital dilemma but by letter received yesterday from old college friend Chloe who, despite malaria, has been working in Mozambique teaching children, digging wells on her day off, and running adult literacy schemes in the evenings.

Close eyes and make urgent offer upwards. Oh Lord – forgive me my Adulterous Transgression. I realise now that I only succumbed to adultery out of poverty of spirit. I should have been serving Africa. I felt I must dedicate myself to something and I knew it began with an A.

Let me be stoned to death if Thou insistest, certainly, with pleasure. As a destiny it is not without its attractions, offering as it does oblivion from Britain's economic ills, Privatisation Bills, etc. Incidentally Lord what is Thy view on the privatisation of water? Since water is undeniably Thine and hath been since the dawn of time when even Tory Cabinet Ministers were nought but slimy things with webbed feet heaving themselves out of the primeval swamp. Art Thou behind the recent drought Lord? Art Thou withholding Thy Co-operation?

But back to Africa. As a teenager I had a crush on Kenneth Kaunda as I am sure Thou rememberest, since I prayed every night for Thee to contrive me an introduction to him. This was in the days when he had vertical hair and wore leather jackets. How I longed to rush to Africa Lord and serve his emergent nation. Where did I go wrong? Was it at Newnham? I expect so.

If Thou wilt turn Spouse into a frog before he can open the door or perchance strike him down – painlessly of course – with temporary blindness, I shall astonish Thee by my devotion to Africa. I shall write no more pulp fiction, a form of literature which I am sure offends Thee. Though the male characters do often possess the imperious attractions and flashing eyes of Thyself in Thy Old Testament mood.

I shall sell all the shameful household paraphernalia of our Pharisee life. How right Thy Runcie was on this point! The video will go first but I will save the duvets if Thou dost not mind, after all it is nearly November. Duvets apart, this little corner of Cranford Gardens will pursue a Third World lifestyle of rice and water and the rest of our income will go straight to Oxfam.

Yea, I shall even send off my lover Tom to Africa with a single chaste kiss on his brow. He will devote himself to plumbing thingies such as wells. He could help Chloe, my friend who labours in Thy vineyard in Mozambique, and who shames me with her altruistic energy. Let not Tom look forbiddenly on her Lord or at least let me never get to hear about it if he does.

But no! I shall also go there. It is not too late to offer my life to Kenneth Kaunda. And I shall take back all the tribal artefacts I bought at that little shop off the Tottenham Court Road.

I shall lie down at dusk on an earth floor wearied from honest toil Lord and rise again at dawn to help plant a variety of crops to nourish the indigenous population. After my midday handful of mealie meal I shall teach the delights of appropriate technology or perchance Congreve's *Way of the World* or whatever Thou deemest needful.

And at my life's end I shall crawl away like an old elephant and die in the shade of one of the many thousands of trees I have planted. Let my bones be picked clean by Thy vultures: fit destiny for a foul Adulteress. Only conceal from my husband the terrible truth! For an entity who created the world a little job like that should be a pushover. Amen. Or as my friend Alice would say – Awomen.

forty-five

FLINCH IN EXPECTATION OF key in lock, but instead doorbell rings. Hesitate. Is it not Spouse, then? Or has he forgotten key, too? Tom enquires, by means of eloquent gesture, whether he should hide in the dining room, but I am unable to reply as I have turned into pillar of salt.

Doorbell rings again, and ex-military voice booms 'Mrs

Domum!' Throw open door and bestow quivering smile upon next door neighbour Mr Twill bearing enormous marrow. O thanks Lord Thou art a Real Brick.

'I just wanted to give you my big one,' he beams, then catches sight of Tom loitering furtively in shadows of hall. I tremble towards utterance.

'This is my . . . plover.'

We all fall silent at this ornithological conundrum.

'*Plumber*,' I affirm. 'I've been having trouble with my S-bend.' Twill commands me never to summon plumber again as he will gladly give my S-bend a good seeing-to whenever I wish. Express gratitude.

Twill presents me with largest marrow ever seen in Western Hemisphere. Promise I will make good use of it and privately wonder if, in present climate of détente, need for fall-out shelters has completely evaporated. Twill departs with roguish wink and further tiresome references to my pipework.

Slam door gratefully on outside world but before amorous negotiations can resume, am arrested by thought that though it was not Spouse that time, he could return at any moment to reclaim briefcase. Tom understandably irritated by this possibility.

'Let's go over to my place, then – the van's just round the corner.'

'But suppose he comes back just as we're walking down the path together?'

'Well why shouldn't we be walking down the path together?'

Not sure if blameless relationship with plumber could include walking down the path together. Most elementary social habits now beyond my understanding, lost in a fog of guilt. Despatch Tom to van and promise to follow after decent interval. If *decent* right word, which doubt.

Van vibrates excitingly through Rusbridge. Tom stops at GREEN LIGHT, new wholefood shop, and nips in to buy something for lunch. Whilst waiting in van, think complacently of the many professional and domestic duties which will await my attention in vain all day.

BLISS'S
WONDER

Must remember to pick children up from school, though. TEARFUL TOTS WAIT IN VAIN FOR TOYBOY-TOUTING MUM. 'Henry and Harriet Domum were found crying by the dustbins behind Rusbridge Co-op last week whilst their mother, romantic novelist Dulcie Domum aged forty-one, frolicked in a love nest in Porritt Gardens with a toyboy fifteen years her junior.'

Tom returns with two Zenburgers already spreading vast oilslick through recycled paper bag. Van leaps asthmatically into life. Wonder if the age gap really is fifteen years. Study Tom's profile as impartially as possible and detect promising laugh lines at corners of mouth.

'Stop looking at me like that or we'll crash.'

Must avoid crash. Must also avoid having children taken into care. (Though tempted.)

Tom declares himself deeply touched to have been described as my plover and promises to peck me to death in the love nest at Porritt Gardens as soon as we get there. Delayed by interminable traffic jam caused by men in Day-glo jackets digging large hole in road, in exactly same place where large hole was dug only three weeks previously. Perhaps one of them dropped a contact lens. Fall silent as have already said too many foolish and fond things for one morning.

Eventually van escapes jam and Tom offers 1p for thoughts. Am obliged to confess that I thought the woman who just walked past looked rather like a girl I had known at school. Tom glad to hear that my mind is a white hot furnace of amorous fantasy. Actually it was a lie. Was really marvelling that, despite the banquet of delights offered, for once, by real life, all my subconscious could come up with last night was another erotic dream about Norman Tebbit.

forty-six

MRS BODY'S MOTHER-IN-LAW, otherwise known as Tracey's Gran, dies in the middle of *Neighbours*, revealing herself as a woman of sensibility. Spouse unable to refrain from observing that Mrs Body's body will soon be a-mouldering in the grave. Recall, with misgivings, that what attracted me to Spouse originally was his wit.

Harriet plucks me by the sleeve and whispers, 'Mummy, what will Tracey's Gran do now she's dead, if she wants to go to the loo?' Explain that loo becomes unnecessary – one of the many benefits of death. Beyond time-share salesmen, too.

Do not intend to join the elder Mrs Body in Limbo quite yet, though. Have got into nice little routine of Life Class every Thursday night and several naughty lunches a week, now Harriet is full-time at school. Naughty lunches usually wholefood take-aways eaten in Tom's friendly old nest of a bed. Wholemeal pastry in my opinion more suited as building material than sustenance, but never mind.

Next naughty lunch, however, in country pub The Trout as Tom has big job on in nearby Pratworth Hall. In meantime persevere with Truffaut season on Channel Four. Cannot help feeling Truffaut's real talent lies in dessert: the conjuring up of trifles, and that what I want from cinema screen is more like roast beef. Mere beefcake, in person of Gerard Depardieu, not enough. Though addition of Depardieu to ingredients would certainly improve any film, or indeed trifle.

Go to bed wishing I could have bestowed an extra twenty years' active life upon Bunuel and Jane Austen. Have frightful dream in which Elizabeth Bennett marries Mr Darcy, loses a leg, plays the piano in the nude and is pursued by flock of symbolic sheep from room to room of vast Baroque mansion. Awake fatigued, and wonder about damage done to subconscious by education.

Eventually weekend shudders into oblivion. Perk up at thought of dear Tom snatching hour to gaze into my eyes over ploughman's lunch at The Trout. Whistle theme from *The Trout* as drive with carefree panache towards Pratworth. Autumnal tints splendid, and pub cosy. Choose seat next to blazing log fire with back to light. (When alone in Tom's attic recently, found his passport and discovered that when he was born I was already at Grammar School, doing Domestic Science – in vain, as it turned out.)

Order large glass of dry sherry and feel its warmth penetrate toes, making up for rather painful new shoes. Scrutinise ankles. Fairly sure they at least are untouched by time. Toes, however, dreadfully mangled. Cannot understand why smallest toenails have turned to quartz and wish they would become pink and smooth again.

Pub fills up. Chaps in tweeds. Expect Tom delayed by Lord Pratworth. Some detail about old lead piping. Order glass of white wine, forgetting head like sponge. Must not drink any more as have to drive home and collect children en route. Lurch to bar for peanuts. Return with nonchalant air of woman enjoying deliberately solitary lunch, but bark shin on chair.

Clock's fingers whizz round to 1.45. Palpitations. Fat bald man asks if he may join me, with unpleasant leer. Give what I hope is curt nod, though double chins seem to go on flapping forever.

Order ploughman's lunch. Appetite has been replaced by anxiety: bread by kapok, Stilton by soap. Fat, bald man asks if it is not a bracing time of year. Feeling urgent need of bracing and hear myself laughing loudly to show how relaxed I am. Order large Perrier and hiccup mournfully for half hour whilst fat bald man laments Nigel Lawson.

Mentally remove five stone of body weight from Lawson and discover he could become Mr Darcy. Worthwhile project for his retirement: profit not profiteroles. Stagger out to car park as it is 2.30 and, alone in car, ambushed by silly tears.

Have been stood up. Possibly because of Pratworth heiress: Caroline, or Charlotte. Drive eccentrically back to Rusbridge. Answerphone winks cheerfully but it is only Mrs Body excusing herself from work tomorrow because of the funeral. Wonder if this might be right moment to make arrangements for my own.

forty-seven

Eventually phone rings, but Spouse, most uncharacteristically, and possibly only to be a nuisance, picks it up. Bury head in cookery book and try to look indifferent. Harriet asks if she can play with flour and water and have answered YES before realising full catastrophic implications of request.

Spouse snaps, 'Wrong number!' and puts phone down. Emerge from tiresome details of How to Make a Salmon Mousse – something, thank God, I am old enough never to attempt – and await, not too eagerly I hope, vital details of Wrong Number. Spouse picks his nose silently and reads instructions on tin of soup.

Clear throat guiltily. 'There seem to be a lot of wrong numbers these days . . . ?'

'Some idiot asking for the Gliding Club.'

At which words, small invisible firework display takes place in my lymphatic system, for Gliding Club is clandestine coded message that Tom has rung. No doubt to explain absence from lunch date. Last few hours of hell replaced by soupçon, or possibly even mousse, of bliss.

Unless of course he rang to say, 'Sorry it's all over – I have fallen irrevocably under the spell of the Hon. Caroline of Pratworth Hall.' Or even worse – her mother. Do not mind bowing out gracefully in due course to make way for pretty young thing who will keep Tom more or less contented, but perhaps not quite amused or stimulated enough to wipe out all pangs of longing for yours truly. Bowing out to youth OK. But could not bear usurpation by another matron. Especially, somehow, a Younger Older Woman.

Am assailed, on way upstairs, by worst thought of all: that it really was someone trying to ring the Gliding Club. Sneak into bedroom to ring Tom from there, but aware that Henry in next room doing something internecine with Action men. Also aware that when I ring from up here, phone in kitchen will utter faint but treacherous PING. Put head round Henry's door and suggest he launch bombing and strafing raid on kitchen and if he can keep it up for five minutes I will give him 20p. Henry astonished but game, and Boldly Goes.

Dial Tom's number. He answers immediately, and begs forgiveness *vis-à-vis* lunch date, but there was a Nasty Situation at Pratworth Hall involving incontinent old plumbing and priceless seventeenth-century Flemish tapestries. Assure him I enjoyed delightful lunch with handsome fellow who explained EMS to me.

Tom silent for a split second. Then 'Are you winding me up?'

Delight at this evidence of his jealousy only slightly undermined by linguistic unease. Wish he had said something rather more pre-war. References to Winding Up can only convincingly be made by persons born since 1960. And even then . . .

Thrust aside these irritating philological quibbles, and listen instead to the gusts of his breath into mouthpiece. Wish I could feel them on my neck. Tom's big job at Pratworth will take all week. Would I like to try a lunch at the pub again or should we wait for Life Class as usual on Thursday evening? Feel I cannot attempt another pub lunch without loss of something or other so say Life Class will be fine. Not sure if Tom disappointed, and if he is, not sure if I am pleased therefore. Replace phone with horrid feeling that I am enveloped by The First Cloud.

Descend to kitchen to find that Henry has bombed and strafed Harriet in the midst of her flour-and-water activities, with horrific consequences. Spouse is ignoring them and is opening a tin of soup with an expression on his face which clearly suggests It Really Is Intolerable That a Man of My Breeding and Education Should Have to Resort to Warming up a Tin of Soup However Gourmet. Realise that when it comes down to it he would rather have married someone capable of making Salmon Mousse, but then so would we all.

'What sort of person,' seek to distract him, 'would use the phrase, *Are you winding me up*?'

Spouse pauses, licks trace of bisque off finger, and smiles to himself rather unpleasantly before replying,

'A clockwork toy-boy.'

MOCK
TURTLE
SOUP
57
LONDON

forty-eight

FIRST CLOUD EFFORTLESSLY DISPELLED by three hours in Tom's arms on Thursday night, during which repeated references were made to my supposed pulchritude. Nobody has ever called me beautiful before, even in the remote past when I might have been. Although in 1971 Simon Skinner informed me I had a beautiful sensibility. I expect he's a merchant banker by now.

Lying nose-to-nose with Tom endlessly delightful. Too close for proper focus: Tom has only one eye but on him it looks chic. Towards end of blissful evening, both admit we would like a quick blast of Newsnight before I go since world events, for once, almost as exhilarating as adultery.

Watch TV in bed, and toast détente in Aqua Libra, which Tom informs me will restore my alkaline balance. Had noticed that I incline to the acid but had attributed it to earlier existence as azalea. Tom strangely pensive later as he helps me into my holey tights. Confesses that the re-unification of Germany has set him thinking about the very black and hopeless outlook for the re-unification of Us.

Kiss his nose playfully, tell him he is a silly boy, and skip away into the night. On way home reflect this was not a satisfactory response to the problem. Owl flies past headlamps. Wonder if this is an omen. Wonder also if Spouse remembered to put milk and marge in fridge, and if not, whether they have gone off. Depressed at persistent need to think about domestic trivia at times of great historical and emotional significance. Hope Tom is not going to go spongy on me.

On kitchen table, find letter from Harriet to Father Christmas asking for SiNDE DoL or BArBe. Thus, at the age of four, she anticipates narcissistic adolescence. Suppress shudder at the thought of vacuous dolls with long nylon hair, Playboy Club legs and titillating wardrobes of lurex and lace. Why not Action Women dolls of muscular aspect carrying spanners, Treasury despatch boxes or javelins?

Tempted to switch on radio but more empires unlikely to have fallen in last half-hour even in Eastern Europe. Find Spouse asleep in front of TV upon which film revolving around torture and car-crashes offers escape from the anomie of winter nights. Wake him and inform it is bed-time. Spouse badly seized up by snooze and hectors me grumpily about middle age as though I invented it.

Dream about Chris Patten. In mid-caress, I whisper to him, 'What's a quasi-gorgeous fellow like you doing in the Tory Party of all places?' He looks embarrassed. 'To be honest, it was a mistake,' he whispers. 'But once I'd realised what I'd let myself in for, it was too late.' Wake up and wonder if any truth in this. Tell myself it is still dark and therefore night. Glance at alarm clock refutes this. Five minutes only left for free-association.

Wonder why I do not dream about William Waldegrave, who if arrayed in dirty boiler suit would at least resemble Tom. Why do I not dream of Tom himself? Twinge of guilt that, at this most dangerous period in Gorbachev's career, I have withdrawn the support of my fantasies. This thought leads unpleasantly to the reflection that my current *opus* has lain untouched for many weeks: the bodices unripped, the scalding tears unshed. Dread phone call from publisher. Trouble with stream of consciousness is that effluent always rises to the surface.

Get up, prise children away from TV and insist they must be dressed before I can count to forty. Then, on my way to kitchen, see self-conscious envelope lying on mat. Addressed to me in impetuous italic and delivered by hand – by calloused yet infinitely tender hand, as I know all too well. Lock myself in downstairs cloakroom and rip it open.

'Look here, Dulcie,' it begins in frighteningly assertive tone, 'Why don't you just piss off out of it? You know you want to be with me: whatever there was between you and him is over. Don't submit to a life sentence. Come away with me. We could go to France or Italy or anywhere with plumbing. Bring the kids. They could be bilingual. Remember I love you. Isn't that more important than anything else?'

forty-nine

Charlotte Beaminster sat huddled under an old aardvark's skin, stretching out her hands piteously towards a small heap of smouldering faggots. A small and bedraggled rat skittered past. The boughs of the Regenwald were bare: drizzle penetrated her tangled curls and her fine patrician brow was bruised from the hailstorm of the previous week. So this was elopement. A tear ran down Charlotte's cheek as she tried not to think of her beloved bidet, her dear duvet, and her pet marmoset, waiting in vain for her at home at Yeltsinborg.

She had hardly seen Cherbagov all week. He was having trouble with the A.P.L.F. *They all wanted to go off and be liberated by themselves. This was not what Cherbagov had in mind. How could they storm Yeltsinborg Castle, execute – or re-educate – the landowner, Peveril de las Palmas de Santa Cruz, and declare the estate a Repression-Free Zone, unless they stood together? The tiresome political dialectic ran away down the sides of Charlotte's mind, and her thoughts turned instead to her erstwhile husband.*

How was Peveril these days? And why had he not come to claim her? To hack off Cherbagov's head with one blow of the ancestral battle-axe that hung above the huge fireplace at Yeltsinborg? Was he not jealous? Did he not care? Was she not even worth punishing? Had she been disowned in her absence: perhaps divorced behind her back? Perhaps she was free to throw in her lot with Cherbagov – to pledge herself to him in a legal union. Although she was not exactly sure whether you could have a legal union, if you were an outlaw.

And would Cherbagov want a legal union in any case? His manner had been so harsh when he had discovered that she had no experience even of cooking turnips in their jackets in the dying embers of a camp fire. Though she had tried her best to keep their hovel tidy, now it was two inches deep in December mud. Cherbagov was always arguing with the Bagarovs, who had declared their birch tree a Cherbagov-free zone. His caresses had grown more offhand. Some nights he never joined her in the mud at all, but sat up by candlelight drawing maps. At such times Charlotte turned her face to the wall – or rather, the canvas – in despair.

But now she felt a tender hand caress her hair. She looked up, and there was Cherbagov, the bleeding body of a wild creature slung over his shoulders.

'Comrade Madam!' he murmured, with all the intoxicating tenderness of the old days, 'I have killed a wild boar for you, with my bare hands. Tonight you shall eat well. Your pretty cheeks will bloom again. And from its skin I shall fashion you a stout hood and cape to protect you from the winter's blast. Poor creature! Do not be cast down. Tomorrow we storm Yeltsinborg, and you shall see your old home again.' So saying, he pulled her up and clasped her to the pulsating Steppe of his chest. 'Never forget, Comrade Madam,' he whispered, 'that I esteem you. That is all that matters.'

Charlotte almost swooned as a riot of conflicting emotions swept through her. Tomorrow she would see Yeltsinborg again! And Cherbagov esteemed her, after all. Would he kill Peveril? Would Peveril kill him? A surge of blood whirled about her brain as she realised that she, Charlotte, wanted to storm Yeltsinborg. Bearing a weapon. Baring her teeth. She might even kill Peveril herself. But if they decided to re-educate him, she'd leave that to somebody else.

Though vaguely aware that Cherbagov was skinning the boar at the same time as making esteem to her, she did not mind. Time was short, and the sooner she got a couple of pork chops inside her, the better.

The cliché about escaping into one's work, not helpful. Still cannot banish odd sense of horror at Tom's invitation to elope with him to somewhere warm and scenic. Cannot even begin to articulate any kind of reply. Only one thing for it. Shall have to go off to London for the day, and shop till I feel sick.

fifty

SEND HIM POSTCARD OF MALLARD DUCK (non committal – I hope. Wish I knew more about sexual habits of Mallard.) *If only oh if only. Alas, have work crisis involving trip to London will ring when emerged.* Am conveyed to station by Spouse who grudgingly concedes my trip to London knowing full well that otherwise he would have to think about Christmas shopping himself.

On the platform, meet Natasha, nice woman I talked to at the Greenpeace ceilidh last year, with daughter Atlantis, Harriet's age, swaddled in Inca knits. 'Mummee is going to London to buy me a Sindy doll,' boasts Harriet. 'Don't count on it,' I writhe, blushing under Natasha's stern wholemeal gaze. '*I've* got one already!' trumpets Atlantis, at which Natasha blushes back. When train arrives we part, since Natasha rolls her own herbal cigarettes.

Ah! Solitary upon a train in Wiltshire! If Spouse had not insisted on seeing me off, could have bought a *Vogue*, though would have had to hide it from Natasha. Instead read back of newspaper opposite. At photo of euphoric Eastern European face, burst into tears of fragile Mozartian optimism and have to conjure up coughing fit to justify them. Remember Henry, with pre-Christmas guile, packed his Walkman for me, with 'Marriage of Figroll – your favourite Mummy.'

Everyone else on train has radio operator's earphones and I have weedy deaf-aid earpieces. Insert into ears and switch on. Countess's solo washes over me. Tears of Mozartian pessimism flood down cheeks. Right earpiece falls out. Replace it hoping no-one noticed. Cherubino arrives to install bidet. Left earpiece falls out. Recall that in some versions of the story, Cherubino and Countess elope and Countess had child by him. In danger of terminal weeping when, luckily, both earpieces fall out.

Oxford Street convinces me that the Green Party's population policy is not Draconian enough, and wish that I had recently re-waxed my Barbour in order to slide through the melée more easily. In John Lewis's, search in vain for least venal Sindy. Their pert bosoms, endless legs, vacuous smiles and inability to stand up are clear evidence of male fantasy on part of designer. Lurex mini-skirt, pink high heels and flowery earrings sickening. Briefly wish I was doll manufacturer so I could market real teenage doll with puppy fat, acne and scowl. She says *No! Why?* and *Sod Off!* Depart in disgust to *The Place to Eat*, where have arranged to meet old chum Anne who is soon departing for Los Angeles.

We wish to eat Seafood, Salad and Crêpes and discover that this necessitates queuing three times. Wish I had removed one sweater or at least Barbour before queuing, but now too late. Mad Christmas gabble begins to ring in ears, and fear this will become *The Place to Faint.* Eventually re-united with Anne. At least she has the grace not to boast about Los Angeles. In fact she dreads it will be full of Sindy dolls made flesh. Silently we mourn the departure of the Iron Age or whenever it was that women over size fourteen were worshipped. Tempted to tell her about Tom, but refrain as her husband was at Balliol with Spouse, and though suspect they hate each other, cannot depend on it.

Depart promising to visit her in Tinseltown and reluctantly direct my mind towards Aunt Elspeth's Christmas present. Distracted by lust for delicious earrings resembling *Helleborus Orientalis.* Well why not for once? Further detained by rather superb Italian shoes of pink suede with witty little heel. Well why not? Disastrously seduced by marvellously exuberant gipsyish skirt with winking mirrorwork and amusing embroidery. Rather short but legs still passable from the knees down so why not?

Contemplate ensemble in, thank God, small solitary changing room and tactful lighting encourages me to imagine Tom's reaction to this splendour. Feel sure it will console him for my spineless failure to elope. Or, if insane impulse results in elopement, would be perfect going-away outfit. Suddenly recognise vacuous smile on face and with horror behold ageing Sindy doll in looking-glass. O hell. It's written all over my face – *Peccavi.*

fifty-one

TEARFUL MEETING WITH TOM AT which I insist I cannot possibly even think of eloping. This is a lie since I have thought of nothing else for a fortnight and to be honest, was thinking about it even before he asked. For those, alas, cursed with Maternity, the only consolation is fantasy. Or as Mrs Descartes observed, *Cogito Ergo Mum*.

Tom says he expected this reply but knows it is only the last tottering stand of bourgeois decency and will ask me again after Christmas has brought home the full horror of family life. Then he leaps on me. His brimming eyes – egad – I feel my bodice ripped – and another 10,000 years in purgatory are clocked up to my account. Luckily in the magical afterglow Tom makes no mention of balmy southern climes as my entire reservoir of bourgeois decency has ebbed away, exposing for the first time for twenty years the ruined pinnacles of my radical past.

Charlotte Beaminster tucked a pistol in her belt and clamped a Transylvanian hunting knife between her teeth as the A.P.L.F. *advanced cautiously to the edge of the Regenwald. There, shimmering in the ethereal December sunlight, lay Yeltsinborg, the castle to which she had been driven as a blushing bride in Peveril's dashing Porschka. And now, her blood tingled as Cherbagov gave her hand a rough peasant squeeze.*

'Aux armes, Comrade Madam!' he whispered. 'When the moment comes, strike home, and you will be free forever!'

Tears of exhilaration burst from Charlotte's eyes, although she was not sure exactly how she would be free forever if there were to be no servants in the Brave New World. Still, the thought of repossessing her dear bidet quelled all doubts. Cherbagov gave the signal to charge: a convincing imitation of the mating call of the Ukrainian snipe. Charlotte burst from the wood and found, to her excitement, that she could run – just like the Spartan girls in the lithographs.

Cherbagov had chosen the right moment to strike. The servants were away at the Advent Fair of St Alopecia, except for Old Anya in the kitchen, who was, in any case, grandmother to most of the A.P.L.F. *Charlotte knew where Peveril would be at this hour. She cornered him in the sauna, aware that through the steam he would scarcely recognise her in her breeches, boots, and new boarskin hood complete with snout and tusks.*

'Do you know who I am?' she commanded of the pale cringing figure on the misty bench.

'Is it you, Boris darling?' came her husband's voice. 'I love that hood! So farouche! Take everything else off and come over here!' So that was why Peveril had never bothered to rescue her. He was a povta. But wait! Cherbagov had taught her to respect all sexual inclinations. Even those of her husband. But still, there was her mission. Charlotte raised her knife.

'Die, Peveril!' she cried. 'And may the monstrous apparatus of patriarchy die with you!'

'What?' asked Peveril, standing up and seizing a towel.

'I said, "Die, Peveril!"' Charlotte had not expected to have to repeat it, somehow. 'And may –'

'Mummeeee! It's time for the School Fête!' Ah yes. The Fête worse than death, none but the Brave deserves the Fair, as Spouse has quipped a thousand times from the comfort of his armchair, beaming farewell to those forms of life not sufficiently evolved to escape the Christmas Fête – i.e. Self and the kids.

Within the first five minutes Harriet wins 50p and runs off to buy cartload of plastic toys, all broken, which leaves her 35p for Santa's grotto, where she is presented with toy dustpan and brush, and when we arrive home, enjoys housework for a whole two minutes before the novelty wears off. Better than I've ever managed.

'By the way,' Spouse emerges from *The Independent* with placatory smile, 'I suppose I'll have to take the kids up to Elspeth's for the New Year. Give you a bit of a rest.'

Reflect that at New Year will be able to elope to Porritt Gardens for a day or two, if I survive Christmas – which without SAS training, unlikely.

fifty-two

'MUMMY,' ENQUIRES HARRIET ANXIOUSLY, 'is Mrs Thatcher real?' Much speculation recently about the existential status of Santa Claus, Jesus, etc. Reply yes, though retain private doubts as to whether Mrs T. is fully biodegradable. Harriet turns pale at the news that the PM is not just another terrifying old witch from a fairy tale.

Cannot bear to think about approaching festivities. Have assembled ingredients for The Dinner, though mincemeat, pudding and Christmas cake deeply unpopular with us all. Spouse remarks unhelpfully that of course Home Made mincemeat etc. would be a completely different experience. Still, he is taking the children to Kirkwhinnie for Hogmanay where they can wallow in Aunt Elspeth's Home Made everything whilst I . . . but do not permit myself to imagine naughty idyll at Porritt Gardens. Must check present list first.

At least confident that Spouse will enjoy, and probably pick up a few tips from, biography of Hitler. Admire the Liberty shawl for Aunt Elspeth, and wonder if she might be delighted enough to leave it to me in her will. Though Spouse says Elspeth defies the idea that You Can't Take It With You and will join her ancestors wearing her best tweed and Celtic silver and clutching the two cut glass decanters he has always coveted. The Nefertiti of Kirkwhinnie.

Am gloomy about presents for the children. Not sure that tasteful ceramic nativity set will console Harriet for non-appearance of Sindy doll. As for Henry, nothing short of Middle Eastern arms shipment would satisfy him, and unlikely that acid rain testing kit will divert him for more than five seconds. Still, at least Santa can soak up the blame. Haunted by a fear that I have forgotten to stock up on one of the essentials of life but cannot think what it is. Despite my hatred of commercialism, etc, the thought that the shops are about to shut for several days brings with it the deepest depression.

Spouse to London for some dinner or other. Take kids for last shopping trip but still cannot remember which essential of life we have run out of. Arrive home, carry first boxful in, go out again to car where Henry and Harriet are engaged in the first barney of Xmas, and to my horror hear front door slam behind me. Keys are on kitchen table. Remember that I had always intended to leave spare key with the Twills next door but had never got round to it. Thoughts fly to Tom – he could probably break in through plumbing outlet or shin gracefully up drainpipe. But cannot phone him from Twills as Mr Twill would insist on shinning up drainpipe himself and break femur.

Children excited by crisis and run round the back whilst I vacillate on the pavement. Decide to ring doorbell of house opposite into which rather smart-looking couple, Marc and Elaine, have recently moved. Elaine, wearing kimono and looking wan, answers door. Ask to use phone, but Tom is out. Explain situation to Elaine who though clearly suffering from flu, offers hospitality, tea, TV for kids, etc. Marc is apparently in Madrid or he would be up my drainpipe like a shot. Feel that Mr Twill may be called upon to lay down his femur after all.

Back in street, behold Henry and Harriet waving at me from our upstairs window.

'The back door was wide open Mummee!' they cry. Hope Elaine did not hear this, and carry more boxes of shopping up path.

Half an hour before the shops close forever, realise it is bog paper that we need. Race to Green Light wholefood shop and buy several rolls of recycled. Wonder if it was newspaper before, and wonder which.

Christmas falls upon us. Harriet quite likes nativity set but informs me it is not Baby Jesus but Princess Lucinda. Feel I may be witnessing end of Christian and dawn of Lucindian era. Henry contrives guided missiles from acid rain test kit and launches attack on manger. Two shepherds badly chipped. Security Council resolution passed declaring stable a No-Go area. Wonder if Henry was Herod in previous existence.

Have nasty moment in bathroom before I realise that recycled bogpaper is full of eccentric imperfections. Essential I survive intact until New Year. Though in my case, *intact* is Emeritus.

fifty-three

ENDEAVOUR TO PACK HENRY'S, Harriet's, and Spouse's bags for trip to Kirkwhinnie. Henry complains of stiff neck. If he has flu, that would scotch their Scottish trip and prevent my idyll at Porritt Gardens with Tom. Then thought flashes through my mind that it may be meningitis, whereat am assailed by flood of horror, mortification and guilt. *If only You keep my darlings safe and sound O Lord I will never gaze forbiddenly upon the plumber again.*

Harriet runs in bawling that Henry has shot the angel off the top of the Christmas tree. Henry enters wearing expression of homicidal glee and flourishing carved wooden fish from Mexico (my Christmas present from Alice and Saskia) in attitude of Kalashnikov. Think perhaps his stiff neck due to too much TV yesterday. Wonder if Almighty received my intercession or whether there is the possibility that, like a FAX, it was held up by line being engaged. Ether must be pretty congested these days. Not sure I am quite ready, yet, to be born again.

Take Mexican fish from Henry explain fish is a symbol of Peace, Love, God, etc. Henry enquires what are chips a symbol of? Suggest he asks Great Aunt Elspeth when he sees her tonight. Harriet says she does not want to go to Kirkwhinnie as Great Aunt Elspeth smells funny. Know what she means, but attempt to distract her with thoughts of toffee, shortbread, dollies in kilts, etc.

Wave family off and offer short but urgent prayer to Volvo, Norse God of Travel, to protect them. Endure apocalyptic vision of motorway pile-up. Deranged with grief, my hair turns white. Have it all cut off, though danger of resembling that Scots girl on TV with the unpleasant manner. Muriel something. If hair were short and white, would treat myself to pair of coloured contact lenses – a lacrymose, tear-washed blue. Thus transfigured by loss, I would hurl myself in the Piddle. Or embark on life of selfless Third World development projects in Ethiopia. Wonder if I should be doing that anyway.

Examine bumf received recently from *SOS Sahel*, organisation working in Ethiopia. Photos of women planting trees and smiling optimistically despite their desperate lot. Real progress evidently possible. Tears flood down cheeks at touching spectacle of this optimism, and at integrity of people working for *SOS Sahel* rather than writing Bonkbusters. Run for chequebook, and reflect that cannot help crying whether international news is good or bad. Grateful for boring tales of insider dealings as offer brief respite to ducts.

Speaking of ducts – but must wait till family is safely arrived at Kirkwhinnie before seeing Tom. Must not provoke Norse, or any other gods. Lie on sofa reading old copy of *Vogue* and picking nose in delicious silence. Wonder if this, too, is a sin. By *SOS Sahel* standards, certainly. Write them another, larger cheque.

Feel hungry. Wonder if women in Ethiopia would mind if I have a tin of sardines. Glad sardine tins no longer come with silly little keys. Could never open them properly. Now use ordinary tin-opener. Much better. Attach tin-opener to tin. Narrow ends successfully penetrated, but on the straight, tin-opener gets cramp and drops out, a bit like Steve Ovett.

Make several circuits with same effect. Tin offers narrow glimpse of sardines at each end but no escape possible. Feel fury rising within me like red-hot cobra. All men's fault. Why millions spent on nuclear fission when problem of sardine tins remains unsolved? And how come fish symbol of peace, divinity, etc?

One last attempt – cut finger – tin somersaults – stinking tomato sauce sprayed all over new cream crêpe shirt. (DRY CLEAN ONLY. Should have known.) Cry *You Bastard*, seize meat mallet and clout sardine tin with white hot strength. It flies to the floor, taking several wine glasses with it. Feel better.

Realise I can have long, hot bath without being disturbed or feeling guilty, and have just lowered myself into steaming depths when phone rings. Motorway police? Tom fobbing me off with transparent excuse? Rush, dripping, to phone where unknown person attempts to sell me insurance. Tempted, but fear no policies equal to my dreads.

fifty-four

PHONE RINGS AGAIN. Spouse confirms safe arrival in Scotland. Aunt Elspeth well apart from Glands, and has made a stew. Shudder at the thought of pearl barley and ragged chunks of old, and probably radioactive, sheep. Spouse grimly exhorts me to Have Fun, and rings off.

Heart almost goes out to him for a moment but boomerangs back when phone rings again. 'Hi Dulcie this is Tom there's been a – well not exactly a hitch but well . . . ' Tom's breath roars Telecomically in my ear. Wish could smell it too. Always sweet. 'This friend of mine – he's called Dog actually –'

'*Dog?*'

'Yeah, Dog, well he was christened Dennis, – anyway he's a great bloke really, and he's well he's sort of turned up, I mean come over anyway, of course, only he'll be . . . around.'

Perhaps I should pack my nightie after all. First night with Tom must not be marred by naked encounter with Dog on landing. Despair anew at lack of interesting nighties. Broderie anglaise, Donald Duck and black nylon hypothermals so disgust me that I usually wear old shirt of Spouse's. Not sure if it would be the act of a gentleman to take it to Tom's however.

Do not waste time on tarting-up as Tom apparently oblivious to my flaws even with his glasses on and what's the point of January if not to provide darkness? Besides, am rapidly approaching age when only appropriate ministration would be that of French-polisher. Will eventually mellow into distinguished old bow-fronted chest with drawers.

Arrive to find Tom and Dog eating lentil porridge. Dog immensely tall with black clothes and fingernails to match. He has recently been travelling in Somerset where he experienced visions and enlightenment but not, apparently, much in the way of hot water. He stares deep into my eyes and declares I am a Child of Fire. He can see my aura it's all fiery.

Insist I am Virgo and therefore, if absolutely necessary, an Earth sign, though to see my garden you'd never believe it. Dog insists that I am a woman of fiery destiny. Not sure I like the sound of this.

Wonder if I left the gas on. Must get Spouse to screw smoke-detectors to the ceiling. Or even better, do it myself.

Tom is Water Sign, well well who'd have thought it, and him a plumber too. Dog confides that he himself is all Air, hence his urge towards Abstraction and things spiritual.

After several hours of things spiritual, and many pints of Organic Somerset Hawthorn Tea, begin to tire of Dog and have to repress urge to summon Vet and have him put down. It is almost 3 a.m. Excuse myself and climb stairs which have become extraordinarily steep.

Lurch to Tom's bed and fall face down thereon. Dream I am having tea with the Queen who has mysteriously become Tom's mother but is Terribly Pleased that he has made friends with a creative person – i.e. me. Awoken by furtive attempts to undress my sleeping form. Tom has finally ordered Dog into his basket for the night and is now All Mine. Alas, it is 4 a.m. and for the first time in recent months, feel that a very little of Tom would be more than enough – e.g. about thirty seconds.

Submit to a series of caresses which in normal circumstances would have called forth my soul to dance upon the ceiling. Soul is crumpled and grumpy and not co-operative. Hope one of my more profound groans will be mistaken for ecstasy. Tom strangely energetic. Cannot help thinking that hyperactivity at 5 a.m. a sign of madness. Or – let's be honest – youth.

Awake at 7.30 a.m. (parental habit) with head like concrete mixer. Attempt to sink again into the arms of Morpheus (well Geoffrey Howe actually) but fail. Tom has rolled himself in entire sheet and lies mummified at my side. Dress, and creep out: recalling how I managed regularly to sleep till twelve on Saturday mornings when young. Obscurely satisfied that naughty night was a disaster. Less cause for guilt. Sink, purring with relief, into own empty bed and delicious coma.

fifty-five

SECOND ATTEMPT AT TRYST WITH TOM equally disastrous. Moments after my arrival he is summoned next door by very old man with blighted ballcock and collapsing pipes.

'It just goes on flushing itself, on and on,' his wife tells me over Last Cup of Tea before Water Turned Off. 'I'm afraid it's going to wear itself out.' Detect here relics of Victorian morality.

'Your Tom is a lovely boy,' she beams. Glow at her use of the possessive article. 'Have you got any other children?' Glow replaced by strange invisible wound in chest. Explain, not too indignantly I hope, that I am not Tom's mother nor could I be. This not entirely true. Could just about be Tom's mother had it been More Fun in the Fourth.

Old woman apologises and says it must be the light, though I know to my cost it is not. She says when you get to her age you lose track of the generations. Ask how old she is. Invited to guess: always an irritating request. Old people, like children, seem to want to boast about their age. Hazard seventy-five. She laughs contemptuously and admits to eighty-three. Gasp effusively, congratulate her and tell her she doesn't look a day over seventy-five – though why this should ever be regarded as a compliment, God knows.

Only old person who really looks young is Sir Michael Tippett, who looked twenty-four for his first seventy years and then aged suddenly to about thirty-eight .

Tom still locked in combat with pipes. Return to his house and achieve several centuries of washing-up. Vacuum from top to bottom, with strange sensation of pleasure never associated with housework in own abode. Collect his dirty clothes and look in vain for his washing machine. Then remember young men go to the launderette – an excuse for exhibitionism.

Tom eventually subdues ballcock and returns. But instead of falling into my arms, he surveys newly cleaned house with disapproval. Enquires why I had to clear his bloody place up like a bloody mother or something. Had not ever heard Tom utter *bloody* at all let alone two in one sentence. Thought that as a Buddhist and Vegetarian, he eschewed them. Stung by his ingratitude, remark that I might as well behave like his mother since I've just been mistaken for her. Tom bursts out laughing and then falls onto his bed saying sorry but he feels bloody terrible all over.

Aghast. Put him to bed and administer flu remedies. When he has fallen asleep, tip-toe out. In hall, notice Michelangelo nude on wall and am paralysed by sudden flash of thought: is Tom bisexual? After all, he is a Buddhist and an Anarchist and a Vegetarian so might well go the whole hog. Five years ago would have hoped he was: would be more Shakespearian, etc. But now, feel sick with fear for several seconds. *O Tempora, O Mores*.

Drive home trembling and attempt to restore equilibrium with cup of cocoa and Jane Austen. Disturbed by conviction that she would not have behaved so rashly. Jane Austen provides safest sex of all: hot looks in cold parlours. Tell myself not to worry as I could just as easily fall under a bus tomorrow. The thought of this nice comfortable death quite consoling somehow. What a scenario for the Nineties: Glasnost, Perestroika, and the Angel of Death.

Distracted by the return of Spouse, Henry and Harriet from Kirkwhinnie. Present me with 1,500 piece jigsaw of the Royal Family – a present from Aunt Elspeth. Spouse has aged several years and remarks that he trusts I got a lot of work done. Reply airily O Yes Several Chapters and remember with guilt that I abandoned Charlotte Beaminster on the brink of murdering her vile ex-husband Peveril in the sauna, where they have since languished for several weeks. Must revive them – or at least her – tomorrow, and hope they are not too limp.

Harriet informs me that there is a pile of dog poo on the front path and it looks like a statue of a gorilla. Feel this is extraordinarily poetic of her. Take shovel, bucket of water, and brush, and Go Out into The Dark.

fifty-six

AUNT ELSPETH HAS KNITTED ME A YELLOW MOHAIR JERSEY, in which I resemble vast mutant chick fed on diet of mad elephants' brains. Depressed about elephants. Clearly remember moment when, as a child, I realised that ivory was not a tree. Thank heaven there is no ivory in the house, then have nasty moment beside piano.

Endure, on TV, usual arguments about livelihoods of ivory carvers. Why can't they re-train, along with nuclear physicists and Brazilian ranchers? Glad my own menfolk pursue socially useful work: plumbing and seventeenth-century history. Worried about Henry, though. Fear he is one of Nature's mercenaries.

Gently steer him towards 1,500 piece jigsaw of Royal Family. After two and a half minutes he declares it is too hard, and he wants to watch *Batman*. Promise he does not have to do puzzle as long as he writes to thank Aunt Elspeth for it. Henry insists he thanked her properly in person. Explain that thank-you letters are special: cast luminous glow over wrinkly features, etc. Henry groans and kicks piano. Reprove him, though since I realised about the ivory, feel like kicking piano myself. Say unless he writes thank-you letter there will be no *Batman* ever again, though judging by evidence provided by society at large there will be little else.

Instantly Henry seizes nearest piece of paper and scribbles *Thank you for the puzzel it is very intresting*. Then races to TV. Feel that, if pressed, he might be persuaded into advertising.

Loiter beside puzzle. Recognise, with strange feeling of achievement, furrowed brow of Mark Phillips. Attempt to re-unite it with his nose but exhaustive search reveals only Prince

Andrew's armpit and the Queen Mum's teeth. Abandon jigsaw and discover with amazement that an hour has passed.

Pick up Henry's thank-you letter and find that on reverse side there is a short lyric poem which goes Library/Tax Disc/Insurance/Tampax/Toothpaste/Bank. ('An economical evocation of the poignancy of homo sapiens' mammalian status, locked within the unrelenting cultural constructs of late capitalism.' – Hilary Spurious.) Clearly, cannot send thank-you letter without sticking it to a piece of card to obliterate shopping list.

Wander off in what I know is futile search for pretty card. Harriet appears and whispers urgently that she thinks she has pooed in her pants. Determined not to give her complex, make light-hearted joke about poo. Harriet launches into interminable series of witticisms on same subject. Cannot work out why forty year olds' jokes on subject are earthy and life-enhancing whereas four year olds' are merely tedious.

Ecstatic force of lavatory flush reminds me of Tom. Wonder if he is better. Just time to ring him before Spouse returns from Seminar on Seventeenth-Century Nutrition. Tom answers in melodramatic croak. Attempt to speak, but am prevented by filament of yellow mohair wound around my tonsils. Utter series of nauseating retches, coughs, hawks, spits and heaves. 'For Christ's sake,' says Tom at other end, 'What's going on?' Replace phone without revealing identity as feel that to do so would be counter-productive. Reflect sadly that this latest attempt to communicate falls rather short of Shakespeare's *On such a night as this*, in which the lovers in the garden enjoy a *sacra conversazione*.

At least have excuse to throw off the mohair sweater. Spouse rings to say he will dine with colleagues as Seventeenth-Century Nutrition more promising subject than he thought. Hopes I am not inconvenienced. Warble O No it was only Mushroom Bake. Short silence as Spouse thinks this is evidence of rare culinary exertion on my part. Actually bought it at *Green Light Food to Go*. Spouse apologises again. Unusually conciliatory. Suspect colleague is female and wish him a jolly evening.

Feed and immobilise children. Then watch fascinating programme about Bald Eagle. Female, reared in Arizona, flies hundreds of miles north whilst male reared in Alaska heads the hundreds of miles south. They meet, understandably exhausted, in Oregon. Perhaps my love life not so complicated after all. Glad I am not a Bald Eagle. Would be sure to choke on mouse's tail. Still, at least the males would have nothing to be anxious about.

fifty-seven

'BUMMY,' HARRIET ADDRESSES ME WITH HER CUSTOMARY CANDLEMAS CATARRH, 'you forgot to wash by face.' Halfway to school, therefore too late. Competent mother would have brought handbag containing Wet Ones. Or have in-car tissues. Or indeed have washed child's face before leaving home.

'I'm sorry, darling. I'm a useless mother.'

'Dough dough you're dot! You're dot a useless Bother!'

Harriet bursts into tears, which in her present Phlegmish state could result in environmental disaster.

Deposit children at school – in Harriet's case, with furtive speed as if planting a bomb – then drive home through Force Nine Gale to hand over car to Spouse.

'This car's filthy,' he observes sourly. 'Inside and out.'

Feel obscurely guilty, as if solely responsible for torrential rain, mud, etc. True, I did allow children to have Fizzy Dippers yesterday, both of which went critical all over back seat.

On entering house, notice that porridge has reached corners of the kitchen hitherto unknown to food, but escape to study hoping that Mrs Body will turn up and mop up. Try not to feel guilty at another wom – er, person cleaning up my mess. Remember it is a Job. But suspect that Mrs Body would be happier re-training as therapist or interior designer.

Charlotte Beaminster hesitated: fatally, perhaps, the instrument of death in her raised fist, her naked ex-husband poised before her in an attitude of aristocratic defiance. Steam hissed and swirled through the sauna. Charlotte's boarskin hood was intolerably hot. A rivulet of sweat momentarily blinded her – and within a second she felt the knife snatched from her hand. She was struck: a chivalrously light but nevertheless compelling blow, which sent her sprawling to the floor.

As Charlotte's fine Grecian nose came in contact with the humid tiles of Carrara marble, and she felt Peveril's foot in the small of her back, she wondered if her return to Yeltsinborg had been foolish. In the forest with Cherbagov she had been free to – well, free, anyway. Now, who knows what torments Peveril had in store? She was his prisoner, without even the creature comforts that had been hers in the early days of her marriage.

But what was this? He was helping her gently to her feet –

Or was he? What the hell is going to happen to Charlotte's husband anyway? Death or re-education? Is re-education of husbands even a possibility? Fear not. Suspect creation of husbands a geological process similar to petrifying well at Matlock. Impossible to introduce new attitudes into consciousness of a husband without resorting to geological hammer.

Break for cocoa. Hope its cultivation does not involve too much environmental and social devastation. Aware that it can lead to eczema, migraine and heart attacks, but manage to draw on unsuspected depths of personal courage and have second cup.

Wonder if Tom is better from flu, if flu it was. Thinking about Tom has become occasional voluntary act rather than helpless surrender to cosmic force. *Love is a constant or still growing light,/And his first minute, after noon, is night.* Expose myself to dangers of third cup of cocoa, and add tears thereto.

Phone rings, and lo! it is Tom. Heart performs sudden violent leap. Could be cocoa, but hope it is passion re-awakening.

'Listen Dulcie, I'm better now – raring to go. Pack your bags. Let's do it. I've got enough dough to get us to Rio.'

Forbear to mention the children. Not sure if eloping would be quite the same accompanied by small girl with deafening catarrh and boy with plastic bagful of NATO aircraft (99p: by-product of détente.)

Ring off with promise to visit Tom at Porritt Gardens and at least watch *Black Orpheus* with him, which he says will do the trick. Gratified to find that passion has indeed awaked, shook its tawny mane and is now prowling through the dark in search of meat.

Must do it. Must not hesitate. Must Boldly Go. Heart hammers, etc. Must kill Charlotte Beaminster's husband. Or re-educate him as interior designer – perhaps a worse fate.

On way back from kitchen, though, am distracted by Royal Family jigsaw and in particular, something odd about Prince Philip's nose.

fifty-eight

HORRIFIED TO READ that methane is one of the Greenhouse gases. If sheep and cows go on burping and farting at present rate we shall soon be out of the frying pan and into the fire. Feel extremely guilty in this respect at having inflicted Henry upon the world. Wonder if sheep could be fitted with catalytic converters. Remember with shudder awful incident in British Museum in 1980 after lunching at *Food for Thought*. Strike beans off shopping list.

Somehow this makes me think of fire alarms. Stand on kitchen table and screw one to the ceiling. After thirty seconds all blood has run out of arms. Lay down arms. Mystified. Thought blood was pumped around body like central-heating system. If pump OK, upstairs should be no problem. Perhaps heart weakened by too much adultery and *News at Ten*. But if blood cannot reach arms when above head, perhaps brain not getting enough oxygen either.

Wonder how Michelangelo managed in Sistine Chapel. Suppose he lay on his back on scaffolding. However did he endure it? But then, he must have been already extremely strange. Michelangelo basically misogynistic. His women all rugby players with teabag tits stuck on afterwards. Transvestites to a man – even in their skin. Shamed by thought of Sistine Chapel, however, and mount table again, but after another twenty seconds' screwing feel faint.

To restore equilibrium, read instructions re fire alarm. Horrified to discover that the device is radioactive. Tempted to send it back immediately, but it was made in Canada, and therefore act of environmental irresponsibility to expose it to mail. Must immobilise it where it is. Feel I should also screw Geiger counter, Radon detector and Methane digester to ceiling.

Spouse arrives from taking children to library. Presents me with large exciting parcel – St Valentine's Day present insists Harriet, at which Spouse utters strange cawing sound. Unwrap it and am confronted with cylindrical appliance resembling handy worktop-size nuclear reactor. Informed it is deep-fryer which will further reduce fire risk.

Children demand we make chips at once. Feel sorry for chips as lid snaps shut before take-off, depriving them of fresh air and daylight as nature intended. Basket is lowered into hot fat by operating handle on outside. Reassured that operation is completed by sound of applause breaking out, as in Wigmore Hall, when chips hit fat. Suspect *chips hit fat* may be anagram of Egyptian deity.

When they emerge, chips have stuck together and are too brown. Children indignant. Spouse tight-lipped. Interesting that my St Valentine's Day present is device for arousing the opprobrium of my family. Escape to study, ostensibly to inspect manuscript, but in fact to phone Tom. No particular message to convey except that I am dying to see him and dreamt we were in Prague last night.

Female voice answers. Thunderstruck. Heart performs triple backward somersault and strange ringing breaks out in head. In arch and hateful voice, make outrageously intrusive enquiry as to the identity of the person answering. Cheerful girlish voice identifies herself as Belinda, friend of Tom's, and can she take a message? Say no, I will ring back later, it's only about my plumbing.

Harriet runs in and says, 'Come quick Mummee it's horrible it won't stop!'

Realise that ringing in ears is external and race to kitchen where fire alarm and Henry are emitting brain-curdling screams. Enquire 'Where is Daddy?' though despise myself for it. Informed that Daddy has taken the chips down the garden to throw to the birds.

Seize screwdriver and leap onto kitchen table. Wish had read instructions properly instead of getting bogged down in the bit about radioactivity. Prise open lid with splintering of plastic. Scream persists. Attempt to lever battery out but seems stuck. Stab wildly at device, then remember radioactivity and scream myself. At final superhuman effort, battery shoots across kitchen and hits Harriet on nose, and we all enjoy two seconds' silence before she starts to cry.

Spouse appears in doorway and asks what the devil I am playing at. Step backwards onto butter. Plate cracks, and it was my favourite.

fifty-nine

HALTED OUTSIDE KITCHEN DOOR AT sound of dialogue within. Harriet: 'ow! Christ! I've banged my farkin' knee!' Mrs Body: 'If I was your Mummy, young lady, I'd wash your mouth out with soap!' Suddenly recall urgent appointment with Royal jigsaw and tiptoe away.

Still something funny about Prince Philip's nose. Whilst meditating thereon, speculate where Harriet can have picked up picturesque vocabulary. Should have heeded Lydia Rainge-Roughver's warning: 'I'm sure Rusbridge primary is a pairfectly naice little school.' Maybe Harriet should have gone off with Emma Rainge-Roughver to be a little Peewit at The Elms. – But no! Still squeamish about paying for a 'better' education, though no qualms whatever about living in handsome Edwardian semi and drinking Aqua Libra instead of council house and Tizer. Suspect that had Harriet become a little Peewit, vocabulary would be just as vile, but accompa-

FOR LINOLEUM WOOD FLOORS AND FURNITURE
MANSION
ANTISEPTIC WAX
POLISH
EXCELLENT FOR THE LEATHER AND COACHWORK OF MOTORS PERAMBULATORS ETC.
FOR LINOLEUM WOOD FLOORS AND FURNITURE
MANSION
ANTISEPTIC WAX
POLISH
EXCELLENT FOR THE LEATHER AND COACHWORK OF MOTORS PERAMBULATORS ETC.

nied by anxious desire to go ski-ing, have live-in Nanny, tall blonde Burberried mummy and black labrador called Jasper.

Realise that Prince Philip's nose is not his at all but that of Mark Phillips. Remove it and apologise for inconvenience. Suddenly hear Mrs Body's shuffle in hall. Seize random book, and stride towards study, flourishing book importantly. Mrs Body ignores me and carries on dirtying hall table with what I trust is the last of the aerosol polish.

In study, discover that book is *Confidential Talks with Husband and Wife* (1900) by Lyman Beecher Sperry, Lecturer on Sanitary Science. Open at random. 'Unfortunately, thousands of careless, selfish and vicious couples do marry, although physically, mentally and morally unfit to bring children into the world.' Close book hurriedly. Feel perhaps I can no longer delay at least brief foray into work.

Charlotte Beaminster felt herself helped to her feet by strong yet gentle hands. Had Peveril then forgiven her betrayals of the marriage bed, her flight to the woods with Cherbagov, her attack on Yeltsinborg with the Anatolian People's Liberation Front? She pushed the boar's head hood out of her eyes and beheld – Cherbagov himself. His frank peasant face was illuminated by its customary integrity, and her small ivory hands felt safe in his. But where was Peveril? Cowering on the sauna bench, his spirit evidently broken by one flash of Cherbagov's commanding brow.

'Oh, Cherby!' she panted. 'Spare my ex-husband – do not have your blood on his hands – let him be re-educated as, perhaps, a people's barber. He was always so fastidious in his toilet. Let this talent be put to the service of the Revolution.'

'Fear not, Comrade Madam,' Cherbagov's manly baritone rang out, 'I shall invite him to form the official opposition.' Charlotte's heart leapt once more at the boldness of Cherbagov's imagination.

Spouse puts his head round door. 'The garden path's a death trap,' he snaps. 'Covered with slime. I'm going to scrub it with bleach.'

Suppress preference for tiny organisms over bleach as know it is futile to argue when Spouse is in the mood for furious hygiene.

Feel pleased with novel. Approaching ending based on freedom, democracy and co-operation. 'A bold new book for a brave new world,' – G. Greene. Move myself to tears at thought of Charlotte, Peveril and Cherbagov co-operating in formation of new Anatolia.

Door bursts open and Henry shrieks, 'Harriet's drunk the bleach!' Blood runs out of arms and legs but still have enough to scream with. Run into kitchen, where Mrs Body is making Harriet drink milk.

'It was very diluted,' says Spouse, 'and she only had a mouthful.' Then he *returns to his scrubbing*. Aghast. Scream 'Where's the Reader's Digest Book of What to do in an Emergency?' Ransack house three times but fail to find it. Ring doctor, hospital and literary agent who all suggest she should be all right with plenty to drink. Race back to kitchen and find Harriet, with beatific smile, making crocodile out of Play-Doh. Apart from swimming-pool flavoured burps, she seems to be OK.

Collapse and request tea from Mrs Body, accompanied by sickening realisation that yet again I have not enough cash to pay her.

sixty

The first day's Congress of the Anatolian Democratic Republic: the lavish domes of St Sinex glittered like Fabergé eggs against the blue sky as the newly-elected deputies streamed up the marble staircase to the Hall of National Reconciliation. Charlotte wondered if her jade linen suit was too ostentatiously plain. Peveril nodded courteously to her as he took his seat as Leader of the Christian Fatherland Party. Charlotte found him an elegant figure in his perfectly cut grey English flannel. She smiled to herself. An aesthetically pleasing ex-husband was an unusual blessing.

Cherbagov's bulky form was clad in a rather shiny example of Anatolian mass-tailoring, but his bright eyes played authoritatively over the chamber and Charlotte's heart still gave a strange little fillip as, for an intimate moment, their gazes interlocked. Of course, as

President of Anatolia, he would have little time for dalliance now. A tear hung in her lashes for a moment as she recalled a moment of ecstasy in a turnip-field, long ago.

Then she banished the quiver from her lip, and unscrewed her pearl-handled pen. She had work to do. No longer did her whole existence revolve around the possibility of a burning glance. She was a person in her own right: the Chairman of the Parliamentary Committee on Women's Education. And as the Deputy for the Districts of Western Amnesia and Porphyry, she was about to move her first motion.

Distracted from apotheosis of novel by arrival of post, including Crabtree & Evelyn catalogue from Aunt Elspeth, with query: do I think Spouse would like present indicated on p48 for his forthcoming birthday?

Object in question is ivory handled badger shaving brush with tortoiseshell stand. For puzzled instant imagine brush is for shaving badgers, then realise with horror that entire animal kingdom is being ransacked for Gentlemen's toiletry requirements. Imagine Harriet apologising to grandchild for disappearance of elephants, tortoises, badgers, etc and offering instead ancestral shaving-brush.

Suspect myself of a degree of hysterical sentimentality. Imagine, as corrective, deathbed of ancient badger, surrounded by ample family of young. Brock recalls sunlit cornfields and luscious blackberries of his youth, and murmurs with his last breath, 'Don't waste me, my children: let me by recycled. I wish to caress the faces of the gentry long after I am dead.' He then expires with a smile on his stripey old face.

Browse through rest of catalogue, and relieved to find many exquisite products made from English Cucumbers. Intrigued by the thought of Swiss Triple Milled Cucumber Soap. Had not realised Swiss had cucumber mills. Would not have thought it possible to mill cucumbers thrice without drowning. Want to buy everything of vegetable or mineral origin. Not sure about sponges and loofahs. Wonder idly if quality of life would improve were I to line my drawers with paper.

This thought leads idiosyncratically to Tom. Reluctant to think of him nowadays as meetings are fraught with impossible demands on his part to leave Spouse and elope with him, taking children if I like. Cannot produce more interesting response than irritated evasion. Yesterday, when I was lying in bath and Harriet ran in and threw a glassful of icy water on my belly, entertained brief wish that Tom would elope with Spouse and children instead. Sigh. Recall there is no fruit in the house, and sigh again.

On way to collect children from school, stop at greengrocer's. Do not think I shall ever conquer my careful aversion for Cape Grapes whatever happens in South Africa. And why, during all the years of supposed economic sanctions, has every greengrocer in Rusbridge offered a positive cornucopia of Cape produce? Dazzled by exotic shine of mango and mystery of passion fruit. Then remember Green Party's exhortation to buy local veg in season and depart with slightly dented swede. Reflect, with deepest sigh so far, that conscience has taken all the fun out of shopping.

Swede delicious mashed with potato and butter, but children revile it in unison. Finally give in to their demands for tinned pasta shaped in form of genetic mutations. Spouse oblivious behind newspaper. Enquire what he would like for his birthday but there is no reply.

sixty-one

Advent of Spouse's and Harriet's birthdays causing some anxiety. Wrestle with conscience as Harriet demands, or perhaps suffers symptoms of, something called Pony Barmey. Well aware that previous Her Little Pony is wedged under pile of tangerine peel and burnt chips at bottom of garden in the hope that, within several millennia, it might biodegrade. Smuggled it hence after hiding it in my wardrobe for three weeks without Harriet's noticing its disappearance.

But alas! Harriet pays a visit to Mrs Body's whilst I am engaged in Last Few Fetid Paragraphs of Bonkbuster, and comes across Tracey's old toys, including entire equestrian establishment in tasteful sucrose-and-nylon. At least have myself transcended the sucrose-and-nylon mode of literary endeavour. Move myself to tears with final paragraphs of Bonkbuster.

Charlotte Beaminster stood on the balcony outside the Tearoom of the People's Deputies, a cup of Comrade Grey Tea at her elbow. A few inches away, also leaning upon the marble parapet, and gazing meditatively down into The Square of Glorious Agricultural Effort, stood Cherbagov. 'It matters not that he is nearly bald,' thought Charlotte. 'And besides, he is only bald on his head. I alone know of the dark thicket on his lower back, like some surviving patch of primeval forest.'

Charlotte recalled the days back at Yeltsinborg when she had come across Cherbagov hoeing, and received an unexpected glimpse of what were to become the Presidential loins. She had not, however, witnessed the birthmark on the buttocks on that occasion. That had been later . . . had it been in the hayloft? Or in the rude sod hut where Cherbagov had secretly studied revolution between the planting and training of mangel-wurzels?

It mattered not. She was translated now into a new mode of being. Passion was, if not spent, at least set aside. And yet . . . Cherbagov turned a strangely feverish glance upon her. For a moment it was as if . . . but surely . . . ? 'Comrade Charlotte,' he murmured. 'Would you care to accompany me to my private quarters? We deserve, surely, a little celebration on this of all days. The Congress is successfully launched. Your erstwhile husband has renounced his title of Peveril St Canonicorum de Las Palmas de Santa Cruz and will henceforth be known as Pev. And you, esteemed colleague, are a People's Deputy. Let us slip away and toast the new order in a bottle of Vroomscht.'

The desire in his eyes was unmistakable. For a moment Charlotte's knees weakened, as they had so often done in the days when he had called her Madam. But no! With a flash of independence she offered him her hand. 'You must excuse me, Comrade President,' she said with a brisk smile. 'Some other time perhaps. Now I have a meeting with some impoverished Kodaks from Eastern Amnesia.' His warm hand closed around hers – perhaps for the last time, perhaps not. And the admiration in his eyes was all the keener for her new independence and spirit.

Charlotte turned on her heel and walked away under the cloudless Anatolian skies. Somewhere, down in the square, a Kapok from Outer Segovia turned the handle of his wheezy old pangolin and the notes of an ancient folksong mingled with the exhilarating hum of the distant bus-station:

'Tis the Eve of St Krill
O come let us wander
Down through the burgeoning birch grove
And gather Snake's Head Fritillaries.

Wonder if this conclusion adequate. Feel tempted to go on and on, like Beethoven. *She sighed. It was over. Or perhaps not. Perhaps this was the beginning. Who knows?* Etcetera. Decide, wisely I hope, to end with Fritillaries. Wonder how they entered my consciousness. Then realise there is a packet of them, shrivelled and unplanted, on the floor of the Futility Room. Only a month or so to go before they flower. Is it too late?

Lurch guiltily to Futility Room where distracted from horticulture by presence of large puddle. Stoop and sniff. Glasses fall off into puddle. Retrieve and rinse. Fetch sponge. Slightly anxious about exact nature and origin of puddle but suspect it is nothing worse than Perrier, so take opportunity of washing the floor with it.

sixty-two

RUSBRIDGE AT LAST HAS ITS TESCO'S. Joined the crowds, all weeping with joy on opening day. Alas, Organic Veg section only three feet square. ORGANIC VEGETABLES sign alone boasted that it was on recycled paper – hundreds of other signs throughout shop presumably on ordinary old tree-murdering card.

As usual when shopping, feel that I am member of a quirky minority which has to be tolerated. Also never more aware of civilisation and its discontents. Cannot even buy bog paper without worrying that it is 100% recycled, chlorine free and undyed. Remember carefree childhood when wiped bum with *Daily Mirror* after having read *Pip Squeak and Wilfred*.

Drive home in post-purchase trance and am met on doorstep by Harriet complaining that she hasn't got a little sister it isn't fair and she would willingly exchange Henry for one. Henry asks if he may have a pet snake. Distract them with Hedgehog crisps (Organic spuds, sunflower oil and sea salt . . . wait a minute, which sea? The North Sea, also known as the Anus Mundi?) Reflect that even cleanest salt not good for children. Tempted to rinse crisps under tap first, but it is too late as they have already eaten them.

After I have unpacked entire three cartons unassisted, Spouse appears in kitchen and complains lugubriously that he will have to go to Winnesota for editorial meeting with the unenlightened Rick H. Dill. Reply that even in Winnesota he will not be able altogether to avoid shopping, and suggest he tries Antarctica instead. Spouse enquires what the hell I mean by that. Nothing my Lord Nothing.

Nothing. Have sent card to Tom saying *Come Let us Kiss and Part* and have heard nothing. Heart now so empty, you can see crumpled old bus tickets at the bottom.

Open fridge and embarrassed by Tofu bought a month ago in a fit of adventurousness. Wonder if it ever goes off. Hope so. Doubt if I could ever get to grips with it. Remove three half-empty pots of pesto, all mouldy. Harriet appears at my elbow and requests that I be a horse. Refuse. She runs off howling and declaring her undying hatred for me. Discover Lego person's footprints in the butter.

Stand up too quickly. Kitchen rocks, sizzles, etc. Henry and Harriet both run in screaming like jet fighters. Spouse appears and enquires if early April would be convenient for him to go to Winnesota. Suddenly his face is replaced by a whirling corona of flashing lights. Brace myself for encounter with Blessed Virgin Mary or E.T. Then succumb to migraine.

Retire to darkened room. Try to ignore stake being driven through eye. Stomach begins to float about. Whole room begins to float about: has become North Sea. Henry comes in and begs me to let him have a snake. Try not to think about snake, but it is too late.

Race to bathroom and spend several minutes retching. Like being possessed. Harriet hovers outside door and worries. 'I don't like your cough, Mummy!' Why can't Spouse round up children just for once and settle down to Snakes and Ladders? – Whoops, snakes again. More retching. But oh no, he has to fossick about in the seventeenth century even at times like this. Feel sure eyeballs have gone down loo, but can still see vague outlines of dirty washing on floor so presumably not. Everything else in body donated to North Sea.

Return, gingerly like damaged cranefly, along landing wall to bed. Sink into stillness. Spouse puts his head round door and asks what he should give children for supper. Reply Your Undivided Attention. He sighs at this unprovoked cruelty and withdraws.

Sometime later Harriet materialises. 'Mummy, I found something on the doorstep.' Gorge rises and forbid further details. 'No, it's nice – look!' Tiny bunch of violets thrust under nose. 'There's a card, too and I can read it,' she boasts. Panic, and urge her to demonstrate. 'It says, *Not Yet*. What's it mean, Mummy?'

'It's all right,' I croak. 'It's only the Milkman.'

Slide into sleep and dream of sea of snakes. Or do I mean can of worms?

sixty-three

ATTEMPT, IN VAIN, TO DETACH BITS OF WEETABIX from yesterday's dried-out breakfast bowls. Leave to soak. Henry asks where his reading book is and demand that I tick the card. Harriet runs in and says she's very sorry Mummy but she has dropped her dinner money down the lavatory. Spouse wonders if I might have time, during one of my leisure moments, to book his flight to Winnesota.

'Leisure moments!' I suddenly screech. Entire family paralysed with shock for split second. 'That's bloody rich! Do I have leisure moments? Do I? Do I? All right, if I have leisure moments I'm going to have one Right Now. You can take the children to school, you can find their reading books, rescue their dinner money, get their snacks ready, fill their flasks with juice, and don't forget the bundle of old tights on the landing for Harriet's teacher to stuff things with. Right? Right. I'm off.'

Slam out of house, pulse racing. Hear faint sound of Harriet bursting into tears in my wake, but harden heart and stride off down hill into Rusbridge. Cannot imagine where outburst came from, but feel wonderful. At same time, tears somehow gathering all round eyes and waiting their chance. Wonder if this is the first Hot Flush, and if so whether I am contributing to Greenhouse Effect.

In Rusbridge market, buy lychees and eat in street. Eating in street probably sign of impending nervous breakdown in over-Forties. Notice new shop selling Tribal Artefacts. Whole shop smells gluey – like those Afghan coats we all used to wear in the Sixties. Am ravished by large wooden Buddha. 'It's from Indonesia,' assistant tells me proudly. Stifle qualm about exploitation and write out large cheque. Promise to return with car, and waltz out of shop beaming, straight into Tom.

Heart leaps at sight of his dear face, and arms twitch with need to throw themselves round his neck.

'Listen,' he says immediately, 'this is no good. What we need is a weekend together. I want to go to bed with you, I want to wake up with you, I want to have baths with you and get dressed with you, I want to kiss you till I'm sick of it.'

At this point Mr Twill walks past, raises his hat, and remarks that Spring has really arrived hasn't it.

Mesmerised by thought of weekend with Tom. Cannot speak. Can only stare dumbly into his eyes and reflect that wooden Buddha cost equivalent of weekend for two in Dorset pub.

'He goes away doesn't he? And leaves you in charge of the kids?' Admit that Spouse is even now girding up his loins for week in Winnesota. 'Well then, for God's sake – tell him you're going off for a weekend. Next weekend. Don't argue. I'll book it. We need it. You know we do. Go home and lay it on the line.'

Part, falteringly, but Tom returns for Parthian shot. 'By the way – you look mind-bogglingly beautiful.' Ah! This is what the tears have been waiting for.

Wander, dazed and weeping happily, into travel agents and buy Spouse his ticket to Winnesota. Assistant seems not to have noticed my mind-boggling beauty. Dismiss financial worries with thought that now I have finished Bonkbuster, should receive second part of advance.

Buy children Whistling Pops to console them for my tantrum. Return to find cryptic message on Answerphone from Jeremy D'arcy: he's finished reading Bonkbuster and loves it, it's marvellous, but *we must talk*. Last four words strike fear into soul as know all too well what they mean.

Children ecstatic with Whistling Pops and destroy their teeth and my brain for half an hour therewith. When Spouse returns, assure him Winnesota flight is booked and then with what I hope is lighthearted aplomb, announce, 'The weekend before you leave I'm going away. If I don't get some peace and quiet I'm going to go bonkers.'

Spouse, clearly recalling morning tantrum, subsides with only martyred sigh. Try to watch news but prevented by firework-display of joy taking place within ribcage. Escape to kitchen. This time Weetabix just floats off like a dream.

sixty-four

CHILDREN MYSTIFIED BY MY DEPARTURE for the weekend. Spouse's frequent absences accepted as a matter of course: but

Mummy, like the poor, evidently expected to be Always With Us. Harriet slightly mollified by installation of wooden Buddha. She insists it is her baby sister Henrietta and dresses it up in an old sun-bonnet. Henry requests that I bring him something back, preferably a computer. Spouse hopes, with clenched teeth, that I will have a good time. Assure him I will.

Tempted to suggest that if Spouse should find himself with any Leisure Moments, he might finish the Royal jigsaw, but refrain. Think it might be pushing my luck.

Drive off in hired Fiat Uno. Experience strange desire to squeak with joy. At Porritt Gardens, furtively collect Tom and then head south, which seems the proper direction for lovers. Sorrento a bit far so settle for Somerset.

Find ourselves in the Brendon Hills. Never heard of them and suspect have entered mythological landscape. Tiny village, whitewashed B&B run by Mrs Thomas, fat friendly woman with two smelly Labradors and blotchy face like a garlic sausage. Exquisite little bedroom overlooking chuckling stream. Tom bumps his head on beam and says it is excellent excuse to spend weekend lying down.

Dusk drives us to The Woodman's Arms. Open fire, gnarled old men carved out of oak sitting on matching settle. Instantly feel trashy, urban, foolish, and apologetic. Old men take to Tom however and when he reveals he is a plumber they break into mysterious gales of mirth. Luckily he does not mention he is Buddhist or Anarchist. They urge him, with scarce-concealed sadism, to try local brew called something like Old Black Stump.

Delicious freedom. Do not have to put old men to bed, clean their teeth or read them stories. Feel brief pang of guilt about children, but conquer desire to ring and say goodnight as know it will only drive Harriet into fit of weeping When are you coming home Mummy when when when.

Back to Mrs Thomas's and up creaking stairs to bed shaped like large soup bowl. Stars above, and stream below, would make it magical even if alone. As it is, am transported. During midnight trip to bathroom, mirror informs me I am eighteen years old. Eventually fall asleep wrapped in embrace. Quite tricky – have forgotten how to do it. Arms keep getting in the way.

Dream that I am in bed with Tom, and door is suddenly flung open revealing Spouse, children and Aunt Elspeth, who pursues me down Rusbridge High Street in my undies crying, 'You dirty girl! You rude girl! You wait till I catch you!' Can feel her breath on my back when am saved – whisked off in Ministerial limousine by Michael Heseltine. He tosses a tawny lock of hair from his brow, fixes me with his sky-blue eyes, and – 'Oh Michael!' I gasp. 'It's been you all along! You have such wonderful hair! Save me from the witch!' Melt into Heseltinian embrace. Awake not knowing where I am nor with whom, but infinitely charmed when truth dawns.

Both our backs have broken in the night owing to steep contours of bed, but never mind. Tom says he was always spineless anyway.

Walk in woods. Carpet of flowers as in Botticelli's *La Primavera*. Pick violets, smell violets, kiss violets. Decorate Tom with violets. Canoodle in area of outstanding natural beauty. Birds sing, sunlight slants, etc. Still think of Michael Heseltine from time to time though. What a strange thing is the human brain. Canoodle in area of special scientific interest. Buds bursting, hearts bursting: tempted to sink down onto carpet of leaves and never rise again.

Eventually drive home and nerve myself for extraordinary step back through looking glass. Henry accepts packet of Polos grudgingly but would have preferred computer. Harriet has arrayed Buddha in old Baby-gro. Spouse evidently exhausted. When I tell him it was Paradise in the Brendon Hills, he says, 'Oh yes – just downwind from Hinkley.' Seems grimly satisfied thus to have put Paradise in its place. And perhaps, to have found excuse for my unearthly glow.

sixty-five

'SWEETHEART!' Tom, newly bold, on phone even before Spouse has departed for Winnesota. 'It was wonderful, right?' 'Right, but, er . . . ' Spouse enters kitchen and enquires irritatingly what he has forgotten. Reply *Just a minute I'm on the phone*. 'Hasn't he gone yet?' Tom sounds as if he plans to come round and send Spouse winging westwards with a hefty kick in the pants. 'No . . . look, I'll ring back.' Harriet informs me that she has spilt her porridge but it was Not Her Fault. Spouse asks if I have any cash. Henry beseeches him to bring back a spacecraft.

'I'm off to work now, but I'll come round tonight,' says Tom, almost menacingly, in my ear. 'And we'll change the locks.' 'OK – I mean, well, not entirely.'

Spouse requests that I drive him to the station immediately or it will be too late. Ring off, unsuccessfully attempting to combine the tender and the brusque, wipe up porridge with tissue, herd kids into car, put Spouse through Passport-Tickets-Money-Pills catechism, then drive like mad to station.

Spouse kisses me briefly on lips. 'They kissed!' yells Harriet in astonishment. 'Ugh!' comments Henry. Spouse looks briefly into my eyes, says, 'Sorry about all this,' and is gone. Odd utterance. Has plangent ring. Is he suffering the premonitions of death customary before crossing the Atlantic? Was it his epitaph? Or has he got more to be sorry about than I realise? Fairly sure his wicked secrets do not include erotic weekend in Somerset with plumber. Obscurely comforted by this thought as I deliver children to school.

Arrive home. Have brief vision of plane plunging into ocean and Spouse's boxer shorts floating poignantly towards Tristan da Cunha. Nose fills with guilty tears. Blow it – alas, on same tissue with which I wiped up porridge. Seek clean tissue to wipe porridge off nose, but box is empty. Kitchen roll also empty. Go into Futility Room and wipe nose on sleeve of gardening jacket.

Phone rings. 'Hi Dulcie this is Jeremy D'arcy can you talk?' Not sure I want to, but acquiesce. 'Look here your book's simply marvellous but I think we need to re-think the second half just slightly, nothing radical, just a change of emphasis. Could you come up and talk sometime in the next few days?'

Agree a date, ring off, and burst into tears. My lovely Bonkbuster! The second half all wrong! And the second half was the *best bit!* Decide Jeremy D'arcy is a stupid git, and wipe nose on teatowel. Heart sinks at having to organise day in London in absence of Spouse: Mrs Body to collect children from school, taxi fare home, Henry and Harriet previously bribed not to say rude words or be horrid, etc.

Spend soothing half hour over Royal jigsaw. Have the feeling that Prince Edward is coming on nicely, though not sure Queen would agree. Strange to think of Tom's visit tonight. Wonder what Queen would think about that. Also wonder how quickly I can get children to bed.

First though, seize vacuum cleaner and embark on orgy of housework culminating in bizarre attempt to thrust whole curtains in washing machine. Someone has wiped their nose on them in the past and fear it may have been me. Recall – too late – fishermen's wives' superstition about not cleaning the house after departure of man for sea.

Henry and Harriet maddeningly reluctant to embrace Morpheus. Endless requests for milk, songs, stories about when I was young, etc. When at last the doorbell rings Harriet yells, 'Who's that? Is it Daddy?' As Tom crosses threshold, two little faces peep around banisters. 'It's that man who can move his hair about!'

In a flash they are downstairs and he is being wonderful on all fours – as only he knows how. Feel momentary pang of nostalgia for Spouse's blast of ire which can send children to bed in ten secs.

Ambushed by fatigue. Sit on too-urgently vacuumed stairs. Try to shake off desire for solitary bed and cup of cocoa and summon up the energy for the wonderful evening which awaits me.

sixty-six

BRACE MYSELF, open fridge and with sickening slosh, scoop entire contents of salad drawer into bucket lined with newspaper. Carry it up garden to toxic dump sardonically known as compost heap. Mr Twill pops up in neighbouring garden and enquires breezily, 'Old Man away?' Affirm absence of Spouse but add, not without dying fall, that he returns from USA tomorrow.

Wonder if Mr Twill has noticed Tom's battered old van parked a hundred careful yards down the road for the last five evenings. Seek to distract him with horticultural blandishments. Remark that I have never seen his ceanothus so far out, so early in the season.

We agree that precocious spring is delightful, though not without sinister undertones *vis-à-vis* Greenhouse Effect. Observe that Political Spring in Eastern Europe also heartwarming though not without sinister undertones either. Cannot understand why first free democratic impulse oft seems to involve beating up other ethnic groups.

Twill agrees it's all very undisciplined. 'What's more,' he booms, 'I do think that Havel johnnie might have got himself a decent haircut before he went to visit Our Queen.'

Interrupted at this point by sudden arrival of Tom around side of house uttering saucy whistle.

'Ah!' says Twill with roguish wink, 'here comes your plumber.'

Tom assumes his professional manner and says he believes I am having trouble with an unpredictable old geyser and can he help. Smile foolishly and beg him to accompany me indoors where I shall be happy to re-acquaint him with my antique pipework.

After only five minutes' re-acquaintance, children arrive back from Mrs Body's an hour earlier than expected, accompanied by the hapless Tracey, who apologises for precipitate return but she has to go to a gig tonight. A band called, apparently, Demented Carrot.

Harriet demonstrates late birthday present from Tracey: male Sindy doll, boyfriend for Gabrielle, female Sindy doll so kindly donated by Mrs Body.

Male Sindy doll ('He's cawed Paw,' Tracey informs us – as in Paw Newman, one suspects) attired in garish Bermuda shorts and fluorescent nylon anorak. Evidently a nine-inch plastic lager lout. Tracey gracefully accepts my feverish thanks and goes off to prepare herself for the Demented Carrot.

'Right!' cries Harriet, 'let's get his clothes off!' Tom smiles at this. 'I know who she takes after,' he says. Harriet looks up. 'What does he mean, Mummy?' Unable to answer. Paralysed by anticipation of naked male doll, knowing verisimilitude of the genre. In the event, privates not visible to the naked eye – as, one suspects, also case with real lager louts.

'I'm going to watch the *Batman* video again,' announces Henry, and rushes off to sitting room followed by Harriet, carrying dolls in naked embrace. Tom and I sit at kitchen table in beautiful evening sunlight and contemplate our last evening together for a while.

'Right, when he gets back,' Tom says seriously, seizing my hand in a way which I suspect I would have found slightly too vigorous even twenty years ago, 'you're going to tell him. OK?'

Squirm slightly and suggest that perhaps Tom is being a little precipitate. Will confront Spouse with inadequacies of the marital relationship, certainly. Probably. Maybe not actually at moment of his return. The next day perhaps or the one after. Would not wish to ruin things by rushing. *Festina lente*.

Tom tosses hair out of eyes with Byronic fervour and warns me that I must grasp the nettle and the earlier in the season it is grasped, the less strong the sting. He then raises my hand to his lips and is just feeding deep upon my peerless eyes when we both hear, in the front door, the unmistakable sound of the Spousian key.

In a flash I am at the other side of the kitchen. I seize the kettle – evidence of innocent domestic activity. Tom rises from his chair and brushes a few crumbs of my skin from his lips.

Spouse enters the kitchen, twenty-four hours early. He is pulled up sharp by sight of Tom, and looks catastrophically displeased.

'Don't say the god-damned S-bend is on the blink again!' he rasps.

'No,' says Tom with dangerous calm. 'It's like this –'

sixty-seven

KITCHEN DOOR BURSTS OPEN and Mrs Twill, face the colour of Persil ad, rushes in screaming, 'Dulcie Oh Dulcie come quick Bernard's collapsed.'

Spouse strides masterfully out as he has Lifesaving Certificate earned by four evenings grovelling on floor of local school having mouth-to-mouth experience with succession of plastic dummies. Recall that Mr Twill has oft rescued me from tricky situations in the past but feel that for him to have a coronary in the line of duty is going a bit too far.

Turn to Tom with face like thunder and hiss menacingly that if he dares to confront Spouse with unpleasant truth about our relationship it will all be over. Tom retorts that if he leaves it to me it will never get said at all will it. Assure him it will, in my own time, in my own way, and if he would be kind enough to piss off immediately I will love him forever.

Tom goes, though dander evidently still erect and tremble at thought of what further madness he may resort to ere it wilts. Then remember that Mr Twill is dying for me out in the garden and rush out with glass of water – pathetic contribution to life-and-death struggle.

Find the noble Twill sprawled beneath his *ceanothus*, deathly pale though conscious. Spouse requests me to ring ambulance. Rush into Twills' house and find phone enthroned upon red plastic pouffe garnished with doily. Dial 999, request ambulance and thank God strike is over. Cannot understand why operator does not sound more excited.

Tempted to loiter in Twillian lounge examining furnishings with snobbish and sardonic eye as do not relish deathbeds especially in flowerbeds. Feel impelled however to assure Mrs Twill that help is on the way. Twill still alive and uttering protests at undignified predicament.

'Dash it, I've peed in my bloody pants, Audrey!' he booms. Assure him that peeing in pants regular occurrence in Domum household, indeed could not respect as human being anyone incapable of it. Mrs Twill shaking visibly and begin to suspect that she, too, is on verge of Beyond. Ambulance arrives promptly and Twill is whisked away, giving orders not to neglect his marrow plants.

Offer Spouse Earl Grey and slice of Dundee cake sent in post by Aunt Elspeth. Spouse annoyed that Mr Twill had not been in need of mouth-to-mouth resuscitation. Has had not opportunity to save a life since the course two years ago. Suspect that had Tom blurted out truth about our liaison, should have obliged Spouse by instant heart attack.

Spouse goes on to remark that though he is equipped to save my life, as I was too bloody lazy to go on the course, he himself would never dare to embark on cardiac arrest without first making sure someone more competent was on hand.

Enquire how was transatlantic co-editor Rick Dill and Spouse says Not Bad After All. Then suddenly, 'What was that plumber doing round here again? What's gone wrong now?' Tempted to say *marriage*, but invent instead strange knocking in the pipes. Report that Tom feels it cannot be solved by mere tinkering: radical re-plumbing only hope. 'He'll be lucky!' growls Spouse.

Henry and Harriet arrive and are aghast to hear that due to their immersion in *Batman*, they missed Mr Twill's heart attack. Henry disappointed that Spouse's gift from USA only a bag of Root Beer Flavoured sweets, not, as anticipated, Space Station.

At bedtime, Spouse comes into bathroom and observes, 'I do realise that any woman worth her salt will have a toy-boy stashed away, but coming back to find him in the actual bed is a bit much.'

Feel skeleton mysteriously turn to talcum powder. Can Tom have scaled drainpipe during evening and installed himself in matrimonial bed? Rush to bedroom and find Male Sindy Doll in Karate attitude on Spousian pillow. Manage, by some heroic convulsion, not to be sick with relief.

sixty-eight

INVITED TO CHILDREN'S BOOKSHOP in Oxford for signing of *Charley the Chickpea* and *Martha the Mung Bean* (miraculously reprinted). Spouse informs me that date of signing coincides with conference he must attend in Exeter. Somehow it is assumed that car must accompany him, though am unclear what even Volvo as old as ours could contribute to dialectic about seventeenth century. This means that I must convey myself to Oxford by British Rail accompanied by Henry and Harriet.

Heart sinks. Cheer myself up by buying long Rainforest Print skirt at local Wholemeal clothes emporium. Don it for trip to Oxford as it discreetly replaces view of bum, hips, and knees with lianas, Brazil nuts and shy peeping endangered species. Offer thanks to Aphrodite for reasonable ankles and cross them elegantly at Rusbridge Station, though without observing any effect on General Public.

Once on train, to buffet, where agonise as usual between Hot'n'Cold Snack or Light Refreshment. Children demand cans of effluent and packets of additives. Guard provides us with dinky little paper carrier to convey edibles back to seat.

Notice that carrier bag sports recycled paper logo and am almost moved to tears when observe that it says *Recycl*ABLE *Paper.* No collection point on train, however: only general rubbish bins. In other words, Joe Public, it's up to you again, mate: fold the bloody thing up, take it home and donate it to your own charity skip on Saturday. Attempt to convey to children my outrage at hypocrisy of British Rail, but without success.

Three hours in Oxford At Leisure as the travel brochures would say. At End Of Tether, more like. Attempt to lead children towards Daddy's old college but they are ambushed by MacDoodle's Hamburger establishment. I am dragged in by the hem of my Rainforest Skirt. Order chicken Macnuggets in limp protest at Brazilian ranching, though not sure this daring piece of agitprop protest quite high-profile enough.

The instant we are seated, Harriet informs me she must have a poo. In crowded but silent Ladies, she declaims:

'Will you please talk loudly Mummy so the people outside can't hear the plop?'

Talk loudly about nice bookshop we will go to, though Harriet plainly bored. Whilst it is my turn to pee, she unlocks the door, and in my haste to get up, tread on Rainforest Skirt and bang head on doorhandle.

On way to bookshop, lured into Laura Ashley and install Henry in corner with comic. Hope its vulgarity will not contrast too harshly with piped musicke (consort of viols) and prevailing air of gentility. Try on ravishing dress but somehow get it stuck over my head and arms and storm about like hysterical mushroom. Harriet refuses assistance. Instead she pulls my knickers down and shrieks, 'I can see Mummy's bottom Henry come and see!!!!'

Escape from dress with slight, and one hopes unperceived, ripping sound, and attempt to interest Harriet in tasteful little sky-blue frock. Harriet inclines to same model in violent pre-coronary pink. Argue for some minutes before succumbing. 'I knew you'd come to your senses,' she observes with satisfaction.

Signing achieved, but return journey turns into nightmare as signals have, as it were, signally failed and entire Western Region is stalled or creeping. Oxford to Rusbridge, one hour in car, becomes epic three hour journey in great tradition of British explorers. At Swindon, ring to inform Spouse of delay but no answer. Then recall he is in Exeter.

Previous user of phone has had effusive experience with can

of Lucozade. Am prevented from treading on Rainforest Skirt by the fact that shoes are welded to floor.

As usual at moments of major discomfort, think of dear Tom. But this time am reminded that I have not obeyed his command to confront Spouse with matrimonial melt-down. Did not even argue very much about his taking the car to Exeter.

Realise that upon arrival at Rusbridge, will have to queue for hours in smoke-filled sentry box for taxi home. Am unhappily aware, as I finally board little local train home, that I have trodden on shy peeping member of endangered species. Wonder if This Means Extinction, and if so, whether I can have some, too.

sixty-nine

PUT OFF, FOR THIRD TIME, appointment with editor Jeremy D'arcy to discuss inadequacies of Bonkbuster. Also delay informing Spouse that marriage is hollow and meaningless, as require him to babysit whilst I attend Commem. at Newnham. Experience frisson as pass through hallowed portals and clearly recall undergraduate conviction that I was there under false pretences and would soon be exposed. Still, comforting to think that in past twenty-five years, some progress has been made in feminist struggle. Tho' forget what exactly.

Observe that we have all exchanged the hesitant bloom of long ago for wrinkles and confidence – with one exception. Scientist from Yorkshire looks even younger now than she did in 1965. Inform her of this fact to which she replies,

'That's an awful thing to say!'

Attempts to communicate with scientists often puzzling.

Would that it were an awful thing to say: would that women, like Sheraton chests of drawers, were more prized with age, our clawed feet and serpentine fronts more admired than the pert aluminium tubes of newer models. Germaine

Greer, glimpsed on High Table, certainly acquiring heroic handsomeness in her middle years, as if her parents might have been Isadora Duncan and Alfred Lord Tennyson.

Dinner light and exquisite: salmon mousse, chicken, and orange salad, thinly garnished with febrile little slivers of peel. Some lucky diners were observed to have been awarded pips, perhaps because they had been exhibitioners.

Self-contained woman opposite, also a scientist, intrigues me. Ask her what she does. She informs me that she and her husband have started a company making the machines that make the machines that make chips.

Charmed by this domestic thought. Well aware of the contribution made to human happiness by the humble chip, and glad to hear that machines to make the machines, etc, are being exported to Japan. Observe that the chip doubtless welcome to a country so fond of seafood. Slight pause, then scientist explains she is talking about microchips. Retire hurt from conversation. It is as I feared: I am here under false pretences and have indeed, at last, been found out.

Speeches. The Principal reminds us that no Newnhamite would ever conform except by choice. Feel guilty as my adult life so far a series of spineless and reluctant capitulations to conformity. Wonder if running off with young plumber would exhibit the right degree of rebellious éclat. Doubt it, somehow. Distracted by Anne Mallalieu's succession of hilarious anecdotes about The Bar and about arriving at Newnham feeling she was there under false pretences, etc.

Then Germaine arrives at microphone like Apocalyptic lion and suggests that any progress on the liberation struggle is illusory. Nay, we are in danger of even letting slip what meagre gains we have made *and not even realising they are gone.* At end of speech another scientist whispers in my ear, 'What was it exactly we were in danger of losing?' Unable to make satisfactory reply.

Journey back to King's Cross not quite comfortable. Though looking forward to a night at Alice and Saskia's flat in Bloomsbury, cannot face intensive all-night dialectic on Germaine's latest salvo in feminist debate. Also, increasingly, hungry, like an old teddy bear who has lost its stuffing and wilts crazily from concave navel.

Arrive at King's Cross at midnight and find Casey Jones still open. Succumb to his musclebound invitation and instruct his Myrmidons to supply me with Chicken-in-a-bun and Chips. Once comfortably stuffed, make game attempt to retain pre-prandial complacency but in vain. Stand meditatively for a moment in King's Cross concourse and watch drunkards chasing pigeons.

'We're soccer hooligans,' confides one cheerful and smiling young man in pink and yellow. 'So next time you read about them, think of us. We're not all bad, you know.'

Assure him I never thought they were.

Walk very fast through Bloomsbury in order to avoid rape, murder and robbery but no-one about. Perhaps all engaged in domestic sex war. Sigh deeply at the thought of returning to my own tomorrow. Dream I am returning to Newnham as student and awake weeping tears of joy.

seventy

CANNOT HELP OBSERVING that though I am a Newnhamite, have not yet been awarded the accolade of a file at M.I.5. Gloomy conviction persists that I have not been nearly subversive enough. Alice and Saskia warn that illicit liaison no substitute for radical political action. Was privately aware of this, indeed regarded it as one of the charms of illicit liaison.

By end of Sunday am exhausted by relentless intellectual debate and would fain have exchanged Alice and Saskia's Bloomsbury pigsty for own provincial pigsty and 107th reading of *Towser and the Terrible Thing*.

Monday: to see Jeremy D'arcy at MaCollins Feldmann (Publishers) Inc. Jeremy indecently young with Rupert Brookean lock of hair and pre-war indolence of manner. Starts by saluting Bonkbuster as 'ahm . . . t'rific fun.' Cringe at this accolade, but suspect I shall cringe more comprehensively ere we are done.

'Erm . . . this Cherbagov guy . . . ' Although location of hackles previously unknown, can feel them unfurling majestically, unimpeded by M&S camisole. 'Look, what with Lithuania and stuff, . . . I'm not sure Gorby's got quite the *cred* he used to have . . . ' Nod in dumb misery.

'And frankly . . . erm . . . I'm not sure the great British romance reader's quite ready for a *bald* hero . . . ' D'arcy tosses own lissom lock out of eye. Hairist! Utter what I hope is majestic, not martyred, sigh.

'Then there's this problem of the Anatolian People's Liberation Thingy. Well fascinating of course to people like us, but frankly erm I'm not all that sure if Revolutionary Politics is as it were the ahm stuff of romance.'

Jeremy D'arcy can patently not remember the Sixties. Bite lip and think of Che Guevara.

'Look, it's just a suggestion, but suppose you make the Cherbagov guy a – erm, say, lion tamer in a travelling circus, maybe a bit taller and, you know, erm, *dashing*, type thing with wild black hair: more sort of Dirk Bogardey. She could run off with the circus, – you know erm, become a trapeze artist or something.'

'And how would it end, then?'

'Well, erm . . . maybe the husband, what's his name? – Peregrine – no, sorry, Peveril – anyway he you know erm goes to the circus one day and that's the very day her safety harness snaps, and she plummets down right on top of him and kills him. But she's unhurt, of course.'

'And the Dirk Bogardey lion tamer lifts her gently off Peveril's crushed corpse, etcetera.'

'You've got it. I mean, it's only an idea. I'm sure you'll think of something better.'

'I doubt it. Thank you. Jeremy.'

On train back to Rusbridge, am required to stand in corridor. After Didcot seats become available but prefer solitary vigil by open window as tears of thwarted creativity have tendency to trickle down cheeks. Also fresh air reviving.

Approaching Swindon am seized by mysterious impulse.

With trembling fingers and beating heart, fling Bonkbuster out of window, complete with Body Shop carrier bag. Experience moment of instant gratification followed by prolonged pangs of guilt. Common pattern of human experience, come to think of it. Wish I could be sure that person finding MS will convey it to recycling skip. O that I had included note to that effect.

Feel moved to jettison much else, starting with Spouse or possibly Tom, or both. Cannot, alas, jettison children – potentially the most life-enhancing move – as find them amusing and inexplicably delicious. Will certainly confront Spouse tonight with inadequacies of Status Quo, and issue ultimatum, as yet undrafted. Will be stern, dignified . . . authoritative.

Moment arrives all to soon. Children asleep, nothing on TV, persistence of daylight forbids early retirement. Am just casting on, prior to knitting brows, when Spouse tosses *Independent* aside, switches on lamp and clears throat.

'My dear,' he says: stern, dignified, authoritative, 'I fear we Must Have a Talk.'

seventy-one

'I'VE BEEN OFFERED A VISITING PROFESSORSHIP at Winnesota,' says Spouse. My brain, poised to plummet down the abyss of A Discussion About Adultery, suddenly becomes a hang glider and launches itself gracefully towards America. 'It was supposed to be Polkinghorne, but he had a heart attack.'

'What? I thought he wasn't even forty.'

'He wasn't. Anyway, Dill's in a jam. He wants me for October, and the poor bastard's so desperate, every time he rings up, he offers me an extra ten thousand bucks.'

'Well I should keep him hanging on till July, then.'

'No. He's got to know by Friday.'

'What about the Department?'

UNITED STATES OF AMERICA
HALF DOLLAR
THE INDEPENDEN
Liverpool cash crisis st

'To hell with the Department.' Spouse has evidently got a galloping attack of Brave New World. 'Collins has been taking me for granted for too long. Let that lazy sod Burton do some work for a change.' Can almost smell the burning of boats. 'How do *you* feel about it?'

Consult my feelings about America, but can only recall heat, lightning bugs, fifty-six varieties of ice cream and – *'Hi, I'm Andy I'm your waider for tonide, and how're yew todaaaaaay?'* – when all one really wanted was, 'The menu, sir.' Urge my brain Westward Ho! with Columbus but it crawls back to hide in the corsage of Isabella the Agoraphobic.

'The kids would love it,' Spouse coaxes. Attempt to imagine Henry and Harriet loving America but instead endure hallucination of my babies assaulted by rattlesnakes, poison ivy, crack-peddling thirteen-year-old hoodlums, TV evangelists, Mothers of Moral America, and lunatic sniper on clock tower of University Library of Winnesota.

'And wouldn't you enjoy escaping for a year from Thatcher's Britain?'

Suddenly, miraculously, it is not Thatcher's Britain any more, but mine. The dripping gargoyles, the thunderclouds over the Abbey, the smell of village shops, the *Today* prog –

'Mama!' from upstairs. 'I dun a poo in the bed!' Race up to find Harriet lemur-eyed in the dark but sheets mercifully pristine. 'It was a dreem,' she decides. 'Mama I dreemed I wanted a poo but all the toilets had changed into soup bowls so I couldn't.'

Feel a piteous pang that my child has been so mercilessly infected with the human condition.

'Don't say toilet, darling – say lavatory.'

'Tracey says toilet.'

'Yes, but – oh never mind.'

Resist Harriet's requests for a Butter Sandwich and *Towser and the Terrible Thing*, and glance briefly into Henry's room. On his bed lies a huge Lego structure which I suspect may prove to be part of a giant gun.

Return to Spouse, who urges me to re-examine attractive prospect of exposing myself upon the anvil of the Midwest to the worst of Winnesotan humidity. What? Abandon the cool intricacies of my own dear grubby nest?

The Goons, the harvest moons, the filthy sea.
The greasy chip bag and the cup of tea:
Lords', Hackney Empire and the RSC,
Bull terriers, Bill Beaumont, Winston Churchill,
My Lady Sneerwell, Tweedie, Julie Burchill.
These cannot be, elsewhere, though you would search all
Continents. For stimulus, for sustenance, for quiet,
From Womb to Tomb I crave my curious diet
Of Save the Steeple, Spot the Ball, and Ban the Bomb,
Of Stilton, toast, Bath Olivers . . . and Tom.
O last and most heart-rending sense of loss!
Worse than the awful end of *Mill on Floss*:
O do not ask it of me, good my liege,
Do not to my most coward soul lay transatlantic siege . . .
But then he spoke, and at his words, my joy was *10 denier* sheer:

'Of course you could be really adventurous, Dulcie – and *stay here*.'

and more . . .

Dulcie Domum returns in More Bad Housekeeping *to the trials, tribulations, turmoils and distractions of 196 Cranford Gardens. Can she cope for a year without Spouse? Can she cope with his return? Read on . . .*

Do you think you could manage the kids on your own for a year?' enquires Spouse.

Heroically refrain from observing that I have been doing just that every year since they were born, and instead demurely suppose I can but try.

'Well,' concludes Spouse, just managing to fight off expression of delirious relief, 'it's a shame, but I think it'll be a lot easier all round if you don't mind staying here.'

Assure him, with stoic dignity, that I do not mind in the least. Manage even at this moment not to think about how much easier it will be, in Spouse's absence, to have my unreliable old pipework seen to by enthusiastic young artisan.

Bask, for rest of evening, in rare glow of matrimonial concord.

* * *

Halfway across country, realise that when Spouse is in U.S.A. for the year, I shall not be able to boldly go to Cheltenham in search of gingham or anything else without first making extensive or expensive child-minding arrangements. Unless I bury them up to their necks in the garden for the afternoon, like play by Beckett. Wonder if Tom would happily take charge for four hours. Suspect he would make excuse about defective cistern somewhere, and depart. We shall see.

Have put myself in training and placed myself on special Single Parent High Vitamin Diet: fizzy Vit.C., Vit. B6, Evening Primrose Oil, Royal Jelly, Beta-Carotene, Brewer's Yeast, Feverfew and Bryonia 6. So should, I hope, be safe from migraine, breast cancer, P.M.T., M.S.E., Nervy and Scurvy. Wonder if it was such a good idea to take so many pills in one fell handful just before I left, washed down with half a pint of newly-opened, high-explosive Perrier.

On way down past pub, appropriately named Air Balloon, emit sudden violent Feverfew-flavoured burp, though uneasiness persists.

* * *

Award myself Earl Grey and teacake, and get stuck into brilliant new novel by Anne Fine. Suspect Anne Fine may be anagram of Irish underground group. Suspect Elizabeth von Arnim may be anagram of Moslem fundamentalist group. Am idling over anagram of Pot of Earl Grey when realise that afternoon is getting on and gingham as yet unsighted.

Distracted as usual by Body Shop. Linger over Juniper and Parsnip massage oil. Wonder if year of single blessedness will include being massaged by young plumber, or whether, as I suspect, massage only occurs in pulp fiction. Buy large number of Body Shop products but only doing my bit for the planet, so no need for guilt.

* * *

Must have bath before going out to buy chicken Raised in Total Freedom, etc. Remove *Datura* from bath (where had placed it last night in vain effort to cheer it up), sluice out bits of compost and run hot water liberally laced with Body Shop Tropical Gel.

Slide therein and, in theory, plan re-write of Bonkbuster. Stare at ceiling and wonder whether Tom will cancel tonight's Life Class too – whether, in short, he is coming to his senses at long last. Unable to shed tear. Fear I am drying out, like that Russian lake, and will eventually become Pillar or rather low, indistinct mound, of salt. Sigh, and wish that I, too, had been raised in total freedom in the forests of France. It's a bit much when one begins to envy the lifestyle of a Tesco chicken.

Eventually get out, and clean bath. Rip up anti-slip rubber mat and – horrors! – find drowned worm trapped beneath, rash emigré one assumes from *Datura* pot. Whole delicious experience of bath ruined. How very Judaeo-Christian. A worm i'th'bath. O worm thou art sick. Evidently, though Body Shop does not test its products on animals, Fate will find a way.

Using loofah, fling worm down lavatory singing brief extract from Mozart's *Requiem*. Feel sick. Too late to go shopping now. Free-range chicken a rip-off anyway. Unscrupulous marketing technique designed to exploit nostalgic longing for gîtes of yesteryear.

And anyway I have planned re-write of Bonkbuster in the bath so afternoon not entirely wasted. The *Datura* can wait another day.

★ ★ ★

Interrupted in middle of my first screen epic by strange stare Spouse is directing at my lower limbs.

'What's happened to your legs?' Inspect them with urgency, as Spouse's expression suggests they may have been replaced by pram wheels à la Saucy Nancy. 'Why so hirsute?' Am dumb. Have not shaved my legs for several weeks: since Tom tenderly enquired 'Why So Prickly?' Have to admit that legs now have rabbinical air. 'Somehow one associates that sort of thing with Poland,' observes Spouse, strolling languidly towards door. 'Pre-Solidarity Poland, in particular.' And with a strange, infuriating, half-amused shrug, he is gone.

★ ★ ★

Next morning, run to Boots. Whilst Spouse is in London, will perform secret trichological rituals. Purchase cream designed to Cover All Grey with Conker Brown, and another cream to bleach legs, already conker brown, a tasteful shade of blonde. Hurry children to bed and ignore Harriet's complaints that she does not feel well. Blame her choice of bedtime story: *The Slimy Book*.

When silence falls at last, unpack mystic creams. Both urge me to test product on small area twenty-four hours before going the whole hog. Sod that. Have bit between teeth, now: squirt gravy-like substance over scalp and secure with plastic bag, then coat legs with bleach cream. Switch on 9 O'Clock News and sit back to wait statutory twenty minutes.

'Mummeee!'

Cannot move: legs are immobilised over white towel in case blobs of cream fall off and ruin carpet. (Clever, eh?)

'I'll come in ten minutes! I'm doing something!'

Then phone rings. Could be Tom. Leap to answer it.

'Can you talk? Listen, why did you piss off the other day?'

Not right moment for in-depth relationship refurbishment. Cannot properly concentrate as I have just noticed that, in my panicky sprint to phone, have scattered little white snowflakes of bleach-cream all over Spouse's ancestral Afghan rug.

'Look – I'm – I'm not quite –'

'Not quite what?'

'MUMMMeee!'

'Wait a minute! – The children aren't asleep yet.'

'Are you O.K.? Is something wrong?'

Something *is* wrong. Legs are beginning to sting. Furiously. God help the animals this stuff was tested on.

'I've got a bit of a headache actually – Ow! Ow! Ow!'

'People with headaches don't say Ow. What's going on?'

'MUMMEEEEE! Who are you talking to?'

'Nobody! – Look I'll ring you back – I've just spilt something on the carpet.'

'I'm coming round.'

'No! Don't! I'm not – not – not in the mood!'

Slam phone down.

'MummEEEE! I feel sick!'

Run upstairs, scattering bleach cream all the way on conker brown stair carpet. Cannot quite get Harriet to the bathroom in time so she is sick on my legs. Quite soothing, actually.